zen
and the
art of
faking it

zen
and the
art of
faking it

JORDAN SONNENBLICK

Scholastic Press   New York

zen
and the
art of
faking it

JORDAN SONNENBLICK

scholastic press   New york

Library of Congress Cataloging-in-Publication Data
Sonnenblick, Jordan.
Zen and the art of faking it / by Jordan Sonnenblick. — 1st ed.
p.   cm.   Summary: When thirteen-year-old San Lee moves
to a new town and school for the umpteenth time, he is looking
for a way to stand out when his knowledge of Zen Buddhism, gained
in his previous school, provides the answer—and the need to
quickly become a convincing Zen master.
[1. Identity—Fiction. 2. Middle schools—Fiction. 3. Schools—Fiction.
4. Zen Buddhism—Fiction. 5. Asian Americans—Fiction.
6. Pennsylvania—Fiction.] I. Title.   PZ7.S6984Ze 2007 [Fic]—dc22
2006028841
ISBN-13: 978-0-439-83707-1 (hardcover : alk. paper)
ISBN-10: 0-439-83707-3 (hardcover : alk. paper)

10 9 8 7 6 5   09 10 11

Printed in the United States of America   23
First edition, October 2007

The text type was set in Gill Sans.
The display type was set in Chauncey DeluxxeBold.
Book design by Marijka Kostiw

To my

darling bride,

melissa,

who has the

patience

of a zen master

a Note
to the reader

Have you ever switched schools? I have, and let me tell you — a school is a school is a school. Every middle school on God's green earth smells exactly the same, because damp lockers, industrial cleaning fluids, and puke are universal. The lunch is the same: How many ways can you flavor a freakin' Tater Tot? The guys are the same: like a show on Animal Planet without the cuddle factor. The girls are the same: Martians with human hormones. And the teachers?

Please.

So when I dragged my feet in their rotting sandals through the gray midwinter slush and up the poured-concrete stairs of Harrisonville Middle School for the first time, I knew exactly what I was getting into.

Sure I did.

welcome to
Nowheresville

So. Eighth grade. Second semester. New state. Math was math — algebra, of course. They always stick the Asian kid in the algebra class. Science was science. Fortunately I know how to roll a stupid little metal car down a ramp and use a stopwatch, so no problemo there. In English, all I could figure out the first day was that the teacher was nuts — so again, same stuff, different time zone. Gym, lunch — I honed my skills at standing *and* sitting in the corner. I also continued my long-standing tradition of eating nothing but pasta and fruit in the cafeteria — I'd never been to a public school that knew how to cook actual meat. Oh, I almost forgot home economics. Brownies. Made with applesauce. No wonder America's kids have lost their way.

It wasn't until the last class of the day that I even woke up. Now, back in Houston, we had been studying U.S. history for the whole year. But in Pennsylvania, for some odd reason, this one school had a special

"Ancient World immersion grant," which meant two things:

one: We'd be spending five months doing the exact same thing I'd done in seventh grade. Well, I guess you can never get enough pyramids, right?

two: I'd miss the whole second half of my country's past. Which kinda stinks — I'd been looking forward to learning how that whole revolution thing had turned out.

Anyhoo, I walked into social studies class alone that day, hovered by the door until I could see which seats would be empty, and then eased my way along the wall and into a chair just as the teacher started clearing his throat to get the class quiet. Lucky me — the chair turned out to be missing half of one back leg. I hit the floor with a lovely *BANG,* and the whole class turned in time to enjoy the view of my books, pens, pencils, and transparent backpack tumbling down all over me.

Yay.

The teacher came hurdling over and reached down a hand to pull me up. I couldn't help but notice he had a twinkle in his eye. An honest-to-God eye twinkle: How weird is that? You hear the cliché all the time, but in this case, it was literally true. The guy had a white beard on a chubby beet-red face and those sparkling eyes. My arm was being yanked out of its socket by Santa Claus. A little pretend voice in my head was telling me, *Stay down! Stay down!* But Santa would not be denied. When he wasn't delivering packages down chimneys, this guy must have worked out like an Olympian.

"Hello, there!" he boomed. Then he paused and twinkled as I tried to be subtle about brushing pencil shavings out of the hair above my left ear. I figured the punch line was coming: "Nice of you to drop in — har-har . . ." Or, "Whoa! Bartender! I'll have whatever this kid is drinking!" But after a beat, all Santa said was, "You must be San Lee. I got a note that you'd be coming some time this week. I'm Mr. Dowd. Welcome to Harrisonville! You came at just the right time. We're starting a new unit today, on . . ."

I tuned out the educational droning and checked out my classmates. Some of them had that look I'd seen in five other states — plus an airbase in Germany — like, *The new kid fell. Cooooooollllll!* Others just looked through me, like, *This new person does not matter in my little Pennsylvania world.* And one girl, with an unruly Aztec temple of brown hair and a Beatles T-shirt, peered over a pair of tiny purple-tinted glasses and gave me a smile that I felt all the way down to my soggy socks. She had these shocking gray eyes that locked right onto mine, angular cheekbones, and super-perfect teeth — which added up to a pretty intriguing look. Unfortunately I got so distracted by Beatle-girl's face that I must have missed a fairly intense death-stare from the guy to her right.

Oh, well. At least there was one human being in this burg. Two, if you believed the friendly Santa guy was for real. I sat down, and class started. Mr. Dowd made everyone copy down a chalkboard full of notes about Buddhism. It looked remarkably like the chalkboard full of Buddhism I had copied down on the first day of a unit back in Texas. I muttered under my breath, "One moon shows in every pool;

in every pool, the one moon." My favorite teacher ever, Mrs. Brown, had said that, whenever I'd commented on how my school in Houston was just like the school before that in Alabama. Evidently it was the kind of thing that Zen masters went around saying in Japan hundreds and hundreds of years ago.

Mr. Dowd was staring at me. "Excuse me. Did you say something, Mr. Lee?"

You had to love his smooth use of the rhetorical question trick. I felt like blurting out, *No, the fat kid in the corner is a ventriloquist and I'm his new dummy. Duh!* But my mom had told me not to draw attention to myself, that this school was the end of the line for me. So I played nicely with others. "No, sir."

He did the twinkle thing again. "That's funny. I could have sworn you'd just murmured a really impressive quotation about the universal nature of reality. Guess it's just the wax buildup in my ears playing tricks on me. Anyway . . ."

As Mr. Dowd launched into what I imagined was a breathtaking lecture on the various branches of Buddhism, I found myself glancing over at Beatle-girl.

She was chewing on the eraser end of a pencil, concentrating intently on Santa Dowd's every word. Come to think of it, so was almost everyone else. Maybe his lecture really was breathtaking. The guy next to Beatle-girl flicked his eyes over to me, and this time I caught the intensity, and the message: *Back off!*

I busied myself with decorating the cover of my new notebook. First I drew three interlocking yin–yang symbols. Then I wrote underneath the middle one, half in outline and half regular: **THE LAUGHING ARCHER.** That was the name of this really cool underground band in Houston that used to play all-ages shows in our neighborhood. The words accidentally filled up the line that said NAME, but since you always put your name in the heading on every page in every school notebook in the world anyway, that didn't seem like a huge problem.

It's funny how innocently things start out.

be
yourself

Before the thing with my dad got really ugly, he used to take me on these little outings. He went through phases, which makes sense in retrospect. So, in Houston, we went bayou fishing in a little flat-bottomed rowboat. In Alabama, it was jogging every Sunday after we got done with services at the Euphrates Baptist Church. Come to think of it, I guess going to the Baptist Church was part of that phase too. In Connecticut, we were Methodists, and I think when I was really little in California we might have been Unitarians for a while.

Whatever, it's easy to get sucked into all the craziness just from trying to describe what happened with my dad, but I'll try to stay on topic — in every state, I've noticed that's the most important thing about writing for the standardized test. So: In California, the phase was archery. Dad and I would load our bows, our quivers full of arrows, and this big collapsible metal easel with a target on it into the back of the Volvo station wagon (or maybe California was the purple minivan), and set off for this gigantic field behind a hunting-supply store. When we first started the archery thing, Dad bought one of those five-color five-circle targets to shoot at. I liked that target, because you got to practice math: The yellow bull's-eye was worth nine points, the red ring around it was worth seven, the blue ring was five, black was three, and the outer white ring was one. You got six arrows, for a high score of fifty-four. This was second grade, and doing all that addition made me feel smart. Also, I was dying to shoot a perfect score, so I was psyched to go every week. I noticed that most of the other guys there had targets shaped like animals, though, and one Sunday when Dad unloaded the easel, our target of circles had been replaced by a realistic portrait of a young male deer. I was pretty displeased with this switch from practicing accuracy and computation to puncturing Bambi, so I asked my dad why we had gotten rid of the old target. He made a sweeping gesture toward all the hairy, grizzled-looking guys surrounding us with their paper zoo of cruelty, and said, "When in Rome, do as the Romans do. Remember that, OK? When in Rome, do as the Romans do."

I could have spoken up, I know. I could have argued the point or begged for my old target back, or something. But even then I knew how my father got if you challenged him. So I turned back toward that easel and started aiming for the lungs.

On my second day of school, I was still trying out who to be in Pennsylvania: a skater, like I'd been in Cali? A Bible-thumper, like I'd been in Alabama? A rich preppy kid, like I'd been in Houston? A macho pretend-jock, like I'd been in Germany? People were always telling kids to be themselves, but either they didn't mean it or they didn't tell you how to go about doing it when everyone else was trying to push and pull you into line.

I was sitting in English class, concentrating on squidging the freezing-cold slush between my socks and my sandals by flexing my toes, when the teacher pinned a badly laminated rectangle of shocking-pink paper above the chalkboard. It was all wrinkly, like she'd accidentally gotten it jammed into the machine sideways, yanked it partway out, and then let it go back through. Come to think of it, that's what her outfit looked like too: the absentminded librarian look. She said it was the Quote of the Day; you could definitely hear the capital letters too. What it said was one of those tired old sayings that pop up in the margins of every middle school agenda book: IF A MAN DOES NOT KEEP PACE WITH HIS COMPANIONS PERHAPS IT IS BECAUSE HE HEARS A DIFFERENT DRUM-MER. LET HIM STEP TO THE MUSIC HE HEARS, HOWEVER MEASURED OR FAR AWAY. I knew from an old English classroom's bulletin board that Henry David Thoreau had said it. I also knew it was the exact opposite of everything my dad had ever told me to act like.

Standing out? Forget about it.

The teacher launched into some long, drawn-out anecdote about Thoreau getting in trouble for his beliefs, which kind of reminded me of my dad. So I tuned out, grabbed one of my notebooks, and started making a list of possible identities for myself. When I had a bunch of candidates, I disqualified each one until my chart looked like this:

Identity	Pros	Cons
– JOCK?	(girls like)	Too much work. Also, I am spaz.
– SKATER?	(cheap clothes)	Too cold. Also, I am spaz.
– PREP?	(good parties?)	Too expensive.
– GOTH?		Mom would kill. Makeup expensive. Also, piercings painful.
– EMO?		See Goth.

Decisions, decisions. I was sick of pretending to be like everyone else — the artificial slang, the Internet research on sports I didn't care about, the endless watching of MTV so I could learn song lyrics, dance moves, cool clothing brands. My dad's way hadn't been working out so well for either of us, plus he was gone. Maybe it was time to pretend something completely different. I didn't actually hear the beat of a different drummer, but maybe I could pretend to be unique.

Be unique? It was so crazy it just might work. But what was unique about me? I was poor. I was Chinese. I was adopted. I had a screwed-up family. I feared bugs, especially spiders. None of those attributes necessarily jumped up and screamed, "LOOK! I'm a STAR!" I tried to come up with some amazing talent I might possess, but because of the whole change-interests-every-year thing, I only had a collection of semi-lame half-talents. And neither "You should see me almost play violin!" nor "Check out my stunning ability to juggle two objects!" sounded like the slogan of a successful middle school maverick.

I thought about it the rest of the day. This was much harder than figuring out how to follow the crowd. Being different, or at least pretending to be different, required creativity. Which I obviously didn't have, or I wouldn't have to INVENT a way to stand out in the first place. Like Beatle-girl: You took one look at her and knew she was hearing a different drummer. Maybe even a different kazoo. For all I knew, she might have been waltzing to the color of a different smell. She was out there anyway.

Example: At lunch in the cafeteria, Beatle-girl had come in two days in a row, dragged a stool over just past the cashiers at the end of the food line, set up an open guitar case in front of her, and started playing a beat-up old acoustic and singing folk songs. And she was really, really good! Her fingers flew over the strings, and her voice rang out sweetly even amid the clanking chaos of the lunchroom. She started both times with a song I'd never heard before, but after the second day it rang out in my head:

> My brothers and my sisters
> Are stranded on this road;
> It's a hot and dusty road
> That a million feet have trod,
> Rich man took my home and drove me from my door
> And I ain't got no home in this world anymore.

In some of the schools I'd attended, Beatle-girl would have been totally ignored. In others, she would have been a laughingstock. In one or two, she might have even wound up with a guitar case full of sloppy-joe goo. But here, some kids stood and watched her act, and some dropped their lunch change into the case as they came off the line.

I was so inspired that on Day Two I even left the safe little corner seat I'd staked out between the chess-geek and clarinet-player tables and walked up to watch. Her hair was a curtain over her face, and every once in a while between lines, she'd try to blow a few strands out of her eyes. Then she'd do a little shrug when the curtain closed over her glasses again.

It suddenly occurred to me that I loved this girl. I mean, her guitar had a gigantic sticker on it that said, THIS MACHINE KILLS FASCISTS. OK, I was admittedly a little fuzzy on what a fascist was, strictly speaking. And I didn't know her name or anything. And she was evidently begging for spare change in a middle school cafeteria. But come on — Beatle-girl kicked serious butt.

Good thing I had probably won her heart by tumbling backward over my own chair at our first meeting. Chicks dig that kind of suave and manly display. Now all

I had to do was talk to her, and she would most likely just melt into my muscled arms. My average arms. OK, my totally hairless, scrawny-chicken-looking arms.

But first I had to figure out who I was this year. And it had to be *good*.

After three songs, Beatle-girl must have realized she needed to spend some of our luxurious twenty-four minutes of lunchtime eating, because she abruptly stopped playing, jumped up, grabbed the coins out of her case, and placed her fascist-killing machine in there. When she was done flipping the little latches on the case, she dragged her stool and the case to the edge of the nearest table. I vaguely attempted to make eye contact, if staring intently at her sandals as she strode right past me into the lunch line counts as an attempt. Hey, she wore sandals, just like me! We were practically cosmic twins!

I was still standing there, near the cashiers, trying to think of a great footwear-related pickup line, when Beatle-girl reemerged from the steamy kitchen with a hideous-looking wheat-type wrap, bursting with massive tufts of bean sprouts. The grim food choice almost forced me to turn my back on her as a potential life mate, but then she redeemed herself by grabbing a pack of chocolate cupcakes from the little shelf at the end of the counter just as she got to the cashier. Interestingly, she paid with a twenty.

Just as I was adding this info-nugget to my scanty store of Beatle-girl data, she looked right at me and spoke: "Woody."

I had no idea how to respond to this, although I tried my best: "Uh, Buzz?"

"No, I mean my name is Woody. You're the new boy, right? In my social studies class?"

I was thinking, *No, I've been here since sixth grade, but nobody noticed, even though I'm the only Asian kid in the whole freaking school!* But I was definitely learning how to bite back the sarcasm, so I said, "Yeah, that's me. San. San Lee."

She just looked at me expectantly, like she was waiting for me to burst into a furious tap-dance number. So I said, "I came here from Houston. Yesterday was my first day."

"Houston? That's interesting. What's it like in Texas? And why did you come *here*? Harrisonville is so boring!"

Now I had a problem. I could agree with her, but diss her town, or I could disagree with her, but avoid insulting her town. This was where not having an identity got tricky.

She must have felt awkward with the silence because she filled it up. "I guess you're kind of quiet, huh? Are you shy?"

She was smiling kindly at me. Hmm, maybe I was shy now. Shy — I kinda liked it. I nodded.

"OK, then, if you need anything — anyone to show you around or give you the scoop on teachers or, well, anything, just ask, all right? This town is pretty lame, but with some expert native guidance, you should do OK. I, uh, better eat now. I'll see you later, San." As she sat down, she did the hair-blow thing again. I don't know why, but for some reason I thought that was the cutest thing in the world.

I wanted to say something witty and smart, but I just kind of mumbled, "Thanks. Uh, see ya."

You know, being shy and all.

Then I walked away, with my hands jammed in the pockets of my baggy California skater jeans, whistling Woody's song.

I was a shy whistler. Not much to pin a whole personality on, but it was a start.

buddha meets
howling monkey

That same day, in social studies, I accidentally added a whole new facet to my pretend identity. Santa Dowd was asking questions about the textbook reading assignment from the night before: "The Spread of Buddhism: China and Japan." Now, admittedly, I hadn't done the reading the night before, but I already knew this stuff. I had even done a whole poster project on Taoism and Zen Buddhism. I've always liked poster projects, mostly because I love the smell of markers.

Even though everyone obviously liked this Dowd guy, of course nobody raised a hand to answer anything he asked. Kids were squirming around, avoiding the dreaded teacher-eye contact, organizing folders, and sharpening pencils that could have already sliced through Kevlar body armor. Woody was looking at me, which caused my big mistake. I wanted to smile at her, but was afraid that would be un-shy of me — so I turned away, right into the twinkly baby-blues of Mr. Dowd. Once he had me in an eye-lock, I knew it was coming. But like a deer in headlights, I was powerless.

"Mister Lee? Can you explain how Buddhism was adopted and adapted in China?"

Huh, I actually did know this. And I was the perfect guy to answer it, since I had been adopted and adapted FROM China. But was I the kind of shy kid who answered teachers' questions, or the kind who crumbled under the glare of full-class scrutiny? Should I mumble "I don't know?" Fall off my chair again? Faint, and hope Woody would seize the opportunity to revive me with mouth-to-mouth?

My eyes flashed over to the new love of my life. She was smiling encouragingly, but didn't necessarily look like she'd be ready to administer CPR if I needed it. So what the heck, I took a stab at answering the question.

"Well, Indian Buddhism was brought to China by traders about, umm, fifteen hundred years ago. The story goes that a man named Bodhidharma was the first Zen master. He and his followers combined the basic ideas of Indian Buddhism with earlier Chinese traditions like Taoism and Confucianism to create Ch'an Buddhism, what the Japanese later called 'Zen.' 'Ch'an' means 'meditation,' by the way."

Had I really just said all that? I guess I had just decided which kind of shy kid to be. I took a breath, looked around, and saw that everyone was looking at me like I had just sprouted a second head. Except Dowd and Woody, who were both smiling. Hmm . . . maybe acting smart had fringe benefits!

Dowd nodded. "Very good, San. Have you, uh, studied Zen before?"

Whoa. On the one hand, teachers usually avoided the topic of students' personal beliefs like the plague. But on the other, I realized that everyone in the room was probably thinking *Chinese kid = Buddhist.* And Woody was still smiling.

I played it cool. "I guess you could say that." A mysterious and knowing half smile played across my lips. Wow, I had a mysterious and knowing half smile!

The lesson moved on, and I answered a bunch of other questions. Near the end of the period, the angry kid — the LARGE angry kid, in case I forgot to mention it — next to Woody leaned across her and asked me in a booming voice, "So, Buddha Boy, if a tree falls in the forest, and nobody is around to hear it, does it make a noise?"

Now, a normal teacher might have jumped all over this guy for blatantly attacking the new kid. But Dowd just leaned back against the chalkboard and twinkled. I hoped his back was getting smeared with fluorescent chalk. On the other hand, I was pleased to note, Woody looked irritated with the smirk the kid was now sporting.

Shy or not shy, I wasn't going to roll over and turn into some steroid case's whipping boy. I replied quietly, calmly, "If a monkey howls and nobody listens, is he still a monkey?"

There was a beat while everyone processed this. Then an intake of breath, followed by a wave of snickering. Two wimpy-looking guys I recognized from the chess table high-fived in delight. Somebody near the front of the room muttered, "Oh, snap! Jones got *told*!"

Felt pretty good until I caught the expression on Woody's face. Now she looked annoyed with me too.

Everyone was looking back and forth between me and the hulking figure of Jones, wondering whether social studies was about to get interesting. But Dowd stepped smoothly into the silence and assigned a chapter to read for homework. Luckily for me, it was more stuff I already knew. This way, if Jones broke all my fingers right after class, I wouldn't have to try turning the pages with a bulky cast on.

When the bell rang, I took my time packing up my backpack. If I scurried out of the room, I'd look like a coward. Well, I was a coward, but there was no need to advertise it.

A shadow fell over me — a wide shadow. I looked up from my fascinating bag-zipping activities, and Jones was leaning over my desk. His massive, veiny arms bulged with power as he put his weight on them. But his face wasn't in "kill" mode. In fact, he had a sort of rueful grin going. Woody and Dowd, who were the only two other people still in the room, looked on with interest as Jones's growl swept over me: "Good one, Buddha Boy. You're pretty funny."

I tried to paste the mysterious half smile onto my face, but I suspect it looked a little bit sickly as Jones punched me playfully in the arm and walked out of the room.

With Woody. Dang.

Dowd said, "You really know your stuff, San. I'm impressed! Your social studies teacher back in . . . um . . ."

"Houston."

"Right. Your social studies teacher back in Houston must be missing you right about now."

I got the half grin up to speed as the feeling began to come back to my arm. I tried not to remember the last time I had seen good old Mrs. Brown, at the courthouse on my last day in Texas. "I don't know, sir. She'll probably survive without me."

"Well, I'm not sure I would have survived this class period without you. Keep it up!"

I walked out of the room, pondering. That was the first time I could remember a teacher ever saying

"Keep it up!" to me without any sarcasm. It felt weird. Possibly good, but weird good.

I mean, are teachers good guys? Mrs. Brown used to let me bring home markers for those posters I mentioned. Dowd twinkled, helped me up off the floor, and actually *praised* me. But then again, teachers gave homework, wrote me up, gave more homework, yelled at kids for being kids all day (Well, *duh*! We *are* kids. . . .), and sometimes even took an interest in their students' lives. Interested teachers had caused me more than enough trouble to last a lifetime.

All in all, it was a tough judgment call and a slippery slope. I mean, if teachers are good guys, then a person might have to decide that cafeteria ladies, school bus drivers, and even — ugh! — assistant principals could be OK sometimes. Which would be a total betrayal of everything I believed in.

Insofar as I believed in anything. I whistled shyly, yet with a certain intelligence, and left the building. My toes had a date with some gray slush.

i become one
with my buddha nature

That evening I made a remarkable decision, if I do say so myself. I actually went beyond a homework assignment. If you're going to be called Buddha Boy, you might as well know enough to fake it. And somehow I didn't think I'd be able to pick up what I needed to know by watching *Total Request Live* or waiting for the premiere of *MTV Cribs: Dalai Lama Edition*. I stopped by my house and left a note for my mom, saying I'd be at the town library. This was a brilliant ploy: First, I wouldn't have to be home for my dad's first scheduled phone call — a huge plus. Second, no mom in the world could possibly get mad at her kid for going to a library voluntarily. She might keel over with a heart attack and expire right there on the ghastly burnt-orange linoleum floor of our apartment kitchen from the shock, but she couldn't be mad about it.

Avoiding angry parents: a definite life skill of mine.

The library was just a block over from our place, so I didn't have far to go, at least. My toes were still clammy and semi-frozen from the walk home. I set out in my sad little Houston Astros windbreaker, which was a year too short on my long, monkey arms and totally lacking in insulation. At least my backpack blocked the biting wind from behind.

Whatever, I got to the library and walked in — a real milestone in my reading career, I assure you. I found an empty table in a dusty corner by the oldest-looking magazines — I didn't want to actually be seen in a library. No matter how smart and shy I wanted to look, I wasn't sure I was ready to go to that length yet. I busted out with the social studies book and read the chapter. It was about the traditions of Zen Buddhism practice, which I remembered pretty well already. First, there were the Four Noble Truths that all Buddhists believed:

1. Life is suffering.
2. Attachment to desire is the origin of all suffering.
3. You can end suffering by giving up your cravings and desires.

4. You can give up your cravings and desires by following the Noble Eight-Fold Path.

I certainly agreed with the first one. Who am I kidding? I was like the poster child for the first one. The second one seemed right too: How many times had I spent months counting down the days until Christmas just so I could get an Ultra-Mega-Transformo-Tron toy? And then the first day back at school after New Year's, some other kid always had the SUPER-Ultra-Mega-Transformo-Tron, and I immediately started lusting after that until my birthday.

Number three sounded like a swell idea. Now that we were virtually penniless, it seemed like as good a time as any to stop wanting things. All I had to do was learn how to follow number four. It occurred to me that this was why I hated research: First, you started out with only four things to learn about Buddhism. Then the fourth one forced you to track down and remember eight more.

I had a sneaking suspicion that the Eighth Fold of the Noble Eight-Fold Path would be something like:

"The key to the Noble Eight-Fold Path is mastery of the Thirty-Seven Lotus-Blossom Precepts."

Wow, I hadn't fully appreciated the advantages of playing dumb until I tried to play smart. After fourteen grueling minutes of book work, my brain needed a break. I had Woody's song stuck in my head and decided to see what I could learn about it; maybe there would be some angle for impressing her.

See? Now I had to do research just to impress a girl. Attachment to desire really *is* the origin of all suffering. I left my book bag on the table and found a computer carrel nobody was using. Just as my mouse-arrow thingy was all lined up on the Explorer icon, a cold-and-bony hand descended on my shoulder. I heard a wheezing inhalation right next to my ear. I swear, it was like Instant Horror Movie.

"Hello, young man," the owner of the skeleton hand croaked. "I haven't seen you around before. My name is Mrs. Romberger. You must have a valid library card to use the computers. Do you have a valid library card?"

No, I felt like saying, *but do you have a valid death certificate? It looks like you'll be needing one any day now.*

But that didn't seem like a very Buddha-esque move, plus I wanted to use the stupid computer. So I smiled wholesomely and said, "Of course I have a valid library card." I didn't tell her that it was for the San Jose Public Library, but that's what she gets for asking vague questions.

I introduced myself and promised not to spend more than thirty minutes on the computer, after which the crone hobbled away to frighten some other innocent seeker of knowledge. Once I got the Internet fired up and my heart back into a normal rhythm, I typed "dusty road that a million feet have trod" into a search engine. I figured that was the most unique phrase from Woody's song, so if the song was at all famous, I'd get some hits. I hit ENTER and pow! Up they came: hundreds of entries.

The song turned out to be from the Great Depression, which, according to the first site I hit, was "a time of great poverty in America that started with the Stock Market Crash of 1929." As far as I could tell from my current financial situation, the Depression hadn't ended yet. Anyway, the song was by a famous folksinger named — get this! — *Woody* Guthrie.

Aha! I had stumbled upon the secret origin of my beloved's name. I read all about this guy. Yeah, he was a guy — the only female Woody in the world was *my* Woody. Anyway, there were like two and a half million search results for his name. He sounded like he must have been pretty fascinating. He grew up in Oklahoma, and his family started out fairly well-off. But his mom started going insane from a genetic disease, his sister died in a suspicious-sounding fire, his dad lost all his money in a real-estate crash, and the family wound up totally broke. Woody ended up homeless and alone as a teenager. Then he learned how to play the harmonica and guitar from street musicians, and started traveling around the country singing about how poor people deserved rights and a helping hand. He wrote "This Land Is Your Land" and over a thousand other songs before he came down with the same insanity disease that had killed his mom.

Oh, and in between there, he was a hero in World War II. He wrote tons of anti-Nazi songs too, and painted "This Machine Kills Fascists" on his guitar. Just like *my* Woody.

His life would have made an excellent *Behind the Music* episode.

I read the lyrics to maybe ten of Woody's songs, enough to get a definite good feeling about the guy and what he'd stood for. I also memorized a few choice quotes, hoping I could reel them off in so-called "casual" conversation with Woody.

One thing about being an eternal new kid *and* having an insane dad: I'd never had a casual conversation, ever.

As I was trying to figure out whether I could somehow get away with printing a few pages of lyrics on the library printer without having to pay ten cents a page, the Ghost of Librarians Past started shambling my way again, tapping her watch.

Yikes! My time was up. I had gotten caught up in the excitement of research. This had been a real day of firsts for yours truly. I smiled, waved, and logged off. Then I realized I still hadn't learned anything about Buddhism beyond what the forty percent of the class that did the homework would know the next day. This gave me the radical idea that perhaps I could take out a book.

But not on my San Jose card. My God! I mean, Jumping Buddhas! Or something. I was going to have to go legit. I went over to the information desk, which was abandoned, and rang this little bell that said RING FOR ASSISTANCE. Apparently in the wacky world of libraries, "assistance" could mean "hot mama." An incredibly beautiful, young-looking lady popped out of a little back room and glided toward me. I felt myself blushing as I cleared my throat.

"Are you . . . um . . . a librarian?" Oops, I hadn't meant to sound so shocked.

"No, I'm a lawn gnome. Yes, I'm a librarian. Well, a librarian in training. My name is Amanda."

"Umm, well, I was wondering if you could help me find some books."

"Sure," she said. "Here! I give you . . . some books!"

She gestured in a wide circle at the stacks all around us, then kind of giggled.

Oh, great. Not just a librarian, but a library comedienne. THAT was something the world needed.

"Uh, yeah. I mean, specifically, some books about Buddhism. Zen Buddhism."

"Lucky boy. We do have a bunch of books on Buddhism. It's a special interest of my colleague. Mildred!"

The crone had a name. And expertise. With my usual luck, of course, it couldn't be the hot librarian who was a Buddhism scholar. Mildred came over and grabbed me by the arm. "Buddhism, young man? Is this for a school project? I bet you have Mr. Dowd for social studies, don't you? He's the only person who ever looks at our Buddhism collection. Other than me, of course. Come this way."

Her bone claw grabbed my bicep and yanked me toward the stacks. "Two ninety-four point three," she intoned. "Right this way!" I had to step lively just to keep from getting my arm ripped off. Mildred could really move when she wanted to. I gave one wistful glance back at the gorgeous information lady before I was whirled around a corner.

Mildred took me through various rights and lefts, while the stacks got dustier and the lighting got dimmer around me. Just when I was sure she was getting ready to murder me and file my body under YOUNG-STERS: DECEASED, she screeched to a halt.

"Hold out your arms, San." She remembered my name. Interesting.

Then she started grabbing books off the shelves at eye level and slapping them down onto my forearms. She was talking to herself too, but I couldn't catch much of what she said: *Zen . . . Tao and Te . . . Archery . . . Book of Koans . . . On the Falsity of Dualism . . .*" When I thought that either she had run out of books or she had noticed how loaded up my puny arms were getting, she climbed up on a step stool and stretched her arms up toward the highest shelf. Great. Now she was going to fall off the stool, break her hip, and die. And without her, I'd starve to death while trying to find my way back out of the stacks. She started dropping a rain of hefty hardcovers down upon me, and the height added to the impact.

I felt like explaining to her that I didn't really want to become an expert on this stuff, that I was just shooting for superficial and phony knowledge, but I thought she might take that the wrong way. So I stood there and sweated as the books piled up higher than my chin. Then Mildred looked down at me and said, "Well, that's a start."

A *start*? Yikes! My shoulders felt like they were ripping off my body. At this rate, the scene at the finish would be Mildred and me staring down in horror at my detached arms atop a pile of gory books as jets of bright arterial blood spurted from my shoulder sockets all over the drab carpet.

Well, *that* would establish my uniqueness at school, for sure.

Stumpy, the Boy Buddha. It had a nice ring, I suppose. I staggered behind Mildred to the checkout desk and barely managed to get my heap o' Zen onto the counter. Mildred looked at me expectantly, and then asked for my library card — the one I'd told her I had.

"Well," I said, "I don't have one for this particular library, exactly."

"And to which library exactly DO you possess a card?"

"Umm, San Jose, California."

Mildred raised an eyebrow. "But you do live here in town, right?"

"Yes, I just haven't had a chance to get a card yet."

"And how old are you?"

"Fifteen."

The brow shot up again.

"I mean, I'll *be* fifteen. So I'm fourteen. Fourteen."

She sighed. "I wish you had been honest with me before you dragged me all over Creation hunting down all these books, young man. Now I'm going to have to put them all back in their places, because you'll need to come in with a parent in order to get a card."

Well, this was a problem. How was I supposed to become a convincing Zen poser by tomorrow without the books? "Isn't there any way I could get a temporary card and just take out a few books? Please?"

She looked pained. "I suppose for a student of Mr.

38

Dowd's, I can work something out. What if I get all of your information now, and we leave the application and these books behind the counter? We have a twenty-four-hour reserve policy. Then you can come with a parent tomorrow and get them."

By now, there was a line of people waiting for me to check out. I felt like they were all glaring at me. Because, well, they were. I could feel the cold trickles of sweat running down the back of my neck as Mildred waved everyone around me.

"OK, but can I please take out just one or two now? I'll, uh, I'll leave you my social studies book as a hostage."

"It wouldn't be a 'hostage,' young man. I believe the word you're looking for is 'collateral.' But that won't be necessary. Even though you have not been one hundred percent honest with me so far, I have a good feeling about you. And you are researching one of my all-time favorite subjects. So, you may take two of these books — but I get to choose which two you take. And you have to promise to read at least one of them tonight. All right?"

I agreed, and Mildred started sorting the books into several piles. Then she handed me a very fat book and a very thin book. The fat book was called *The Zen Garden,* and the thin one was called *Sitting Zen: Meditation in Practice.* I thanked her and apologized, and thanked her again. I also pledged to read one of the books. I would have given her a pint of blood if she'd asked for it. I had to get pretend-enlightened, and fast; Mildred was my new hero, bony hands and all.

As I shoved the books into my bag and headed out, I took one last look back over my shoulder. Amanda the Hot Library Comedienne had magically appeared again, and was leaning over and stacking my books on the Reserve shelf behind the counter. I'd be back. The library was way more interesting than I'd imagined.

Sadly, so was my arrival back home. My mom was home from her job as a nurse at the hospital and refused to believe I'd really spent several hours at the library without her having dragged me there and nailed my feet to the floor of a carrel. I explained the whole thing to her. Well, except the Woody research part. And the hottie librarian bit. And the thing with my totally fabricated new personal identity. But the woman was just naturally suspicious, which was peculiar since her keen detective sense hadn't stopped her from marrying a compulsive liar psycho like my dad.

This was an extra-intense interrogation session too, because I'd missed Psycho Dad's call. She started in with a whole lecture: "You should have been here, Sanny (Yuck! She truly does call me that. . . .). Your father can only make the one call a week, and it costs a fortune. Now he has to wait all week again to hear his son's voice. He's dying to know how you're adjusting to your new environment."

I hoped he was enjoying the bread and water in *his* new environment, the sleazebag.

"But mom, I was 'adjusting to my new environment' by studying. The kids here are way more advanced than the kids were in Houston."

She squinted at me, like her special brainwave-vision would reveal the truth behind my library excursion. "Really?"

This was, in fact, the truth. Plankton were more advanced than the kids in our subdivision outside of

Houston. When I'd been there, some extremist preacher had declared our suburb an "Evolution-Free Zone." I thought he was declaring the obvious, about a million years too late. The only thinking adult in the whole burg was Mrs. Brown, but one great social studies teacher wasn't enough to drag a whole town kicking and screaming into the age of standing totally upright and speaking in sentences.

"Yeah, really. And I want to make a good impression here." Again, totally truthful. "Now, if you'll excuse me, I have to read an entire book on Zen Buddhism before bed." This was yet another accurate statement, although I didn't tell her I'd be reading a *short* book on Zen Buddhism before bed. What kind of lame-o teenage boy would pick a long book about gardening over a short book on sitting? Sheesh, I sat all freakin' day at school, and I used to sit even longer after school before we'd been forced to sell off my Game Boy and the family Xbox. I had a feeling a book on sitting would be playing to my strengths.

She let me go, even though I could tell she was just bursting to ask me another ninety or so questions about my second day in the "new environment." Invoking schoolwork is a powerful parent-repellant tool; you just have to use it sparingly so that you're not forced to perform too much actual schoolwork.

In my room, I plunked down on my narrow and saggy bed, taking a split second to mourn the memory of my old extra-wide waterbed from California. Then I took another second to grieve over my pawned iPod: "O iPod! Pod that you were! I have lost you! Gone is the smooth pinch of your earpiece. Farewell, my faithful dispenser of noiseful bliss!" Et cetera.

I'm a great procrastinator, or at least I'd always prided myself on being one until this fateful moment. I opened the *Sitting Zen* book, and entered into whole new worlds of procrastinational mastery. These Zen guys were good — they had turned sitting and emptying their minds of all conscious thought into a *religion*! They spent years sitting together in monasteries. People actually got paid room-and-board to sit, sometimes for their entire adult lives. And all this time, I'd been doing it strictly on a volunteer basis.

Well, now it was time for this amateur to go pro.

Sitting master,
freezing rock

I got to school early the next morning, so the weak winter sun was just beginning to peek over a line of storefronts and onto the big lawn across the street from the school building as I found my sitting spot. It had to be conspicuous, but not too conspicuous. My dad had always told me, "Don't look like you're trying. The best actors *never* look like they're trying."

And I had to admit, right up until that bad day in Texas, my dad's acting skills had been a hit wherever we went.

So I found a big, flat rock under a leafless, snowy tree directly across from the school's front walkway and sat zazen. That's the posture you always see in karate movies, where the guy's legs are crossed over each other so that each foot rests on the opposite thigh and the hands fold over each other to make a little oval between the thumbs and the edges of the palms — kind of like he's pouring a small, invisible cup of water forward over his ankles. I was facing sideways so that the arriving students would see me in profile, at a distance, silhouetted in front of the rising sun.

Maybe I should be a movie director when I grow up.

I had about twenty minutes to kill before everybody started pulling in, so I swayed back and forth until I was comfortable like the *Sitting Zen* book said you're supposed to. Then I tried to breathe deeply and evenly until I forgot about breathing. Do you know how hard that is? I tried counting breaths, then I tried NOT counting breaths. But when you're purposely NOT counting, your brain wants to count.

It crossed my mind that if the goal of sitting zazen was to forget about all conscious thought and just be, counting and purposely not counting were equally counterproductive. It also crossed my mind that the followers of Zen might not be enlightened; maybe they were just really, really sleepy.

After a while I did manage to stop thinking about breathing by a clever trick: I concentrated on feeling all the individual molecules of my butt freezing solid, one by one. When my whole butt was completely numb — and I mean novocaine numb — I focused on the numbness. But numbness isn't the same as not thinking; it's just thinking about how you have no feeling in your tushy.

Just when I thought my whole backside might actually crack off and tumble away from my body in a solid block, Woody popped into my peripheral vision. She was getting out of a minivan in front of the school. Jones popped out right behind her. She must have seen me, although I couldn't turn my neck to look without blowing the whole pose. Then she started walking my way. So did Jones. Yikes!

Wait. I was way too Zen — or at least too numb — to say "Yikes!" I was in the zone, or at least I was supposed to be. Let the boy-mountain come to me.

Woody stepped right in front of me, guitar case in one gloved hand. Jones was wearing gloves too. Ha! I spit on gloves. Gloves are for those who have not mastered their inner soul force. Or for those whose moms have money — one or the other. Woody gently laid the case down on the ice-crusted grass, and said, "Good morning, San! How are you today?

You were amazing in class yesterday. I can't believe how much you know about Buddhism!"

"Neither can I," I replied.

She giggled, and Jones grimaced. "So, uh, Peter and I were wondering: What are you doing?"

Ah, it was time for the Zen Show. "Sitting."

"But why?"

"The sun is up."

"What?"

Half grin maneuver: activated. "I like the morning."

Jones — *Peter* Jones — said, "I like the morning too, but you don't see me squatting on a rock. I mean, no offense, but what's the point?"

"Sitting."

Jones was getting frustrated. Goo-ood. "Well, what were you thinking about?"

"I was thinking about not thinking."

I smiled warmly — well, frozenly, but with happy emotion — at Woody. She blew her bangs away from her face — I loved that — and said, "How do you think about not thinking?"

"Without thinking."

Peter Jones rolled his eyes behind Woody's back, and said to her, "Come on, we don't have time for this. We're going to be late. Are you coming, Buddha?"

Woody said, "We'll be in in a minute, Peter. I want to talk with San for a minute."

Peter didn't move, although I think his jaw clenched up.

Woody looked at him with slight scorn: "Alone, Peter." Oh, yeah, baby. That's what I'm talking about. Go, Buddha Boy!

Peter stomped away, kicking up little puffs of sparkling frost. Woody locked eyes with me. "You're so . . . different from everybody else here."

"How do you know? We've only known each other for a day."

She nodded her head toward the crowd that was slowly filtering its way into the two main doors of the building. "Look at them. They're sheep. Small-town sheep!"

Bitterness was not the way to enlightenment. I think I had heard that on a beer commercial once. It was a pretty clever commercial. "Woody, I have only one answer to that."

"What?"

"Baaaaaaaa!"

She looked puzzled, then smiled. "See? You're just so — I don't know — *real*. Now let's go to school!"

I tried to get up, but my butt was both frozen and asleep. I was thinking, *If it's frozen, how can I tell it's asleep? And yet, if it's asleep, how can I tell it's frozen? Hey, that's a Zen riddle! I am getting GOOD! But seriously, I think I am stuck here. I cannot move!* I half smiled half-dazzlingly at Woody and said, "Woody, would you mind helping me up?"

"Sure," she said. "Why else are we put here on this miserable spinning mudball if not to help each other up?"

See why I loved her? See?

She grabbed my right hand and pulled me gently, yet with some oomph, down from the rock. I slid forward and somehow managed to unfold my legs just enough to get them under me so that I only crashed into her a little. "Zen," I gasped through the riot of pins and needles that was suddenly wreaking havoc throughout my lower body, "is not for the faint of heart."

"Neither am I," she purred, and into the school we went. Not a bad start for Day Three, right?

the right
path

In English class, the teacher put this quote on the board for journal time: PARENTS CAN ONLY GIVE GOOD ADVICE OR PUT THEM ON THE RIGHT PATH, BUT THE FINAL FORMING OF A PERSON'S CHARACTER LIES IN THEIR OWN HANDS. — ANNE FRANK. As usual, we were supposed to spend fifteen minutes jotting down our deep and cosmic thoughts about the quote while the teacher checked her deep and cosmic e-mail.

What was I supposed to write about this one? My dad didn't give good advice, he gave evil advice. And my mom gave good advice, but she had wound up as a poor single parent with a felon for a husband, so how much wisdom was I supposed to get from her? And finally, how was I going to form my own character when my role models were total crashing failures? I remember this one time in Alabama, my dad and I were grocery shopping and the cashier was this really nice teenage girl that had always been kind to me. I used to steer our cart to her line every time, because she sometimes even gave me a lollipop. Anyway, my dad let me pay, and she accidentally gave me change for a twenty when I'd given her a five. I realized the mistake when I counted out the fifteen extra bucks in the parking lot, and asked my dad if I could run back in and give the money back. My dad said, "Are you kidding me, Sanny? People are dishonest, and they'll screw you nine times out of ten. So when you get a break, you take it. You don't owe anybody anything." I asked what would happen to the cashier when she didn't have the right amount of money at the end of the day. He said, "What do we care? She was probably dipping into the till anyway. They all are. And if the boss does ask about it, she'll bat her pretty little eyelashes and they'll forgive her. Because people are chumps." I thought about it all the way home, and turned to look out the window so my dad wouldn't see me cry. The next time we went to that store, there was a new cashier. And no lollipop.

"People are chumps. They'll screw you nine times out of ten." My dad was like a satanic Doctor Phil.

My mom was the warm one, like Oprah. She was always saying, "You have to give people a chance." When my dad first got busted, she was like, "It's a mistake. Your father is innocent. You'll see. Your dad isn't the type of person who would cheat anybody. We'll get this cleared up in no time." I was thinking, *Mom, are you nuts? Dad is exactly the type of person who would cheat everybody. He lies just for fun.* Throughout the horrible pretrial period, when Mom had to work double nursing shifts at the M. D. Anderson Cancer Center, and we still had to sell off almost everything we owned just to pay for the hot-shot lawyer dad insisted on, Mom said it was all a mistake. When the trial began and witnesses started flying in from all the places we'd lived with hundreds of pages of evidence — that my dad had sold fake title insurance in Alabama, performed home inspections without a license in California, sold spoiled meat to restaurants off the back of a truck in Dallas while he was supposed to be away for the weekend at a Bible retreat — Mom said it was just a series of misunderstandings. Until the police actually came and padlocked our apartment door shut *with my cat, Sparky, inside,* Mom insisted everything would be OK. But we lost everything. Dad went to prison until at least my twentieth birthday, I never saw Sparky again, and Mom and I wound up in Nowheresville, Pennsylvania, for no apparent reason.

I guess I could have written all of that into journal form, but it might have cast some doubt on my whole Zen image. So instead I wrote:

This quote by Anne Frank is definitely true. According to the traditions of my heritage, karma, or the luck you put into the world through your own actions, is the only thing that determines your fate in this or future lifetimes. So even though my father, for example, might tell me to be kind to those who are less fortunate than I am, ultimately I can do whatever I want with that advice. And then I will have to carry around the results of my actions pretty much forever. Also, a great Zen thinker named Yamada Roshi said, "The purpose of Zen is the perfection of character." And if your parents' values just

automatically made you a good person, nobody would
need to meditate in order to perfect his own character.
As Basho said, "Do not seek to follow in the footsteps of
the masters. Seek what they sought." You need to find
your own way in the world.

English Teacher stood behind me for a while when I'd finished writing, then leaned across me and wrote, THOUGHTFUL ENTRY. KEEP IT UP! under my last sentence. I must say, you can learn a lot from a short little book. I was now looking smart in two different classes. And I could even feel parts of my legs again.

At lunch, Woody only played one song on the guitar before packing up. Then she came over to sit with me at my little leper table. "Hey, San. Are you defrosted yet?"

"I don't feel the cold when I'm meditating." Yeah, right.

"Huh. Uhh, how was your morning? You have Starsky for English first period, right? I do too, third period. What did you write about that quote?"

So I told her the whole thing, and she looked at me all googly-eyed, like I was some kind of Zen master.

D'oh. I asked Woody what she'd written about, and she told me: "I wrote about how my parents are greedy capitalists, and how I'm totally different from them. Like, we have all this money, and other people have so much less. It doesn't seem right that we don't do more to even things out. My dad . . . oh, never mind. You don't want to hear about this."

I leaned toward her and said, "Sure I do. I want to know all about you."

She smiled uncertainly, but started talking again. "My dad's a dentist, so we're basically rolling in it. And one day last year, I asked him if I could donate my allowance to the soup kitchen downtown. He got really mad, and said that if 'those people down there would just get off their butts, they could get themselves a job, no problem. We're living in the land of opportunity, for Christ's sake!' Then he said that since I seemed to feel we have too much for our own good, he would take away half of my allowance until my next birthday. So that's why I collect money at lunch — so I can donate to the soup kitchen without my dad finding out."

And she thought I was the real deal. I wasn't worthy to wash this girl's feet. Fortunately she didn't know that. Which got me thinkin'. "Hey, I've been looking for someplace to volunteer. I miss helping out. Do you ever serve food at the soup kitchen or anything?"

She looked almost scared for a second, and I wondered if maybe she was one of those rich girls who want to help the poor without having to get anywhere near them. "I haven't so far, but I'd love to start."

Do I move fast or what? Before I even opened my delicious Snack Pack pudding (this week's nearly-expired sale item at the local supermarket), I had set up my first date. And my first experience of helping people. I wasn't sure if the good karma of volunteering would make up for the bad karma of being a complete liar.

Oh, well. Zen is supposed to be about living in the

moment, and for one shining moment, I had pudding to eat and a girl by my side. Which reminded me: "Hey, Woody. Do you take requests?"

"What do you mean? Like, will I carry your books to class? Because I'm not into being subservient."

"No, do you *take requests*? You know, when you're singing at lunch. Like, can I ask you to play a certain song?"

"Uh, I don't know — nobody's ever asked me that before. Most kids our age don't like the same kind of music I like, so . . . well, what did you have in mind?"

"There's this great song called 'Hard Travelin',' by Woody Guthrie. I thought since you're named after him, and you played 'I Ain't Got No Home in This World,' you might —"

Her face was glowing as she cut me off in mid-explanation. Wow, I had never made any girl's face glow before. "I love that song! It's the first Woody Guthrie song I ever learned to play. It has this really cool guitar pattern called a Travis pick in it. My guitar teacher says . . ."

And she was off on a happy tear until the lunch bell

rang. She was so ecstatic that she never even asked me how I knew about Woody Guthrie. Of course, I never asked her how *she* knew about him either — which would have been a great move on my part. But I suppose I have no regrets about that conversation; I figure if you could take back the past, my mom wouldn't have worn those hideous polyester argyle sweaters in all of her school pictures, right?

In social studies that day, I was the star of the homework review show. Then we did a lovely work sheet that I totally aced. And next came the best part: Dowd announced that we would be doing a special project on any aspect of Eastern religious tradition we wanted. And when he assigned partners, I found out Woody's last name: Long. Which happened to come right after Lee and before Petrucci in alphabetical order on the class list. So, I WAS GOING TO BE WOODY'S PARTNER IN CLASS FOR TWO WEEKS! Dowd gave out a big sheet of criteria for the project, and then told us to meet with our partners and brainstorm. He didn't have to tell me twice. As I was attempting to appear nonchalant and rush to Woody's side at the same time, I noticed that Peter was off in a corner with some girl named Abby. She was pretty and seemed very nice and friendly, but he was sulking like he'd been sentenced to work for the next ten years with a hunchbacked Nazi.

Whatev. I had some brainstorming to do. Woody said, "Isn't this great? I'm so lucky — I get to work with the expert! We're going to do something about Zen, right?"

"Uh, I don't know. There are so many other fascinating aspects of Eastern relig —"

"You're kidding, right? You have the edge here, San! We have to capitalize on that."

Whoa, this was a new side of Woody's personality: a competitive streak. But then again, I'd only known her for two days. Plus, I had only been me for two days, so how picky could I be about her quirks?

"Uh, sure. I guess that's true. Gotta play to our strengths, right?"

"That's right," she said, blowing on her bangs. "So start giving me ideas, OK?"

Why not? She was certainly giving *me* some ideas. "How about I teach you to meditate?"

"That sounds like fun, but it won't make much of a presentation. No offense."

"Of course not. OK, what if we do a poster project on Zen gardening?"

"What's Zen gardening?"

This girl asked some great questions. And I would even have been able to answer this one if I had just read the fat book instead of the thin book. "Well, it's kind of complicated to explain to the . . . uh . . . Western mind. No offense."

"Try me."

I'd love to. "Uh, maybe when we have more time."

She frowned.

"Wait!" I exclaimed. I mean, I exclaimed it quietly and calmly. Sort of. "I've got it! You want to play to our strengths, right?"

"Well, I want to play to *your* strengths. I don't have any strengths, San."

Was she kidding me? How could someone so

completely beautiful and individual not know about the strengths she had? "Of course you do: music!"

"All right, music. But how is me playing the guitar and singing going to help us with a Zen project?"

"That's for you to figure out."

"OK, then what are you going to do for your half of the deal?"

I had no freaking clue, so I half smiled inscrutably at her. "You'll see."

"When?"

"Tomorrow, Woody. You'll see tomorrow."

Which meant I'd be spending tonight with my good friend Mildred.

not the
true tao

Did you know it's possible to read a book about gardening for two straight hours? Unfortunately, it's not *very* possible. I had two hours to kill after school before my mom would be home from the hospital and I could drag her to the library, so I decided to read the Zen gardening book really fast. After about ten minutes of grappling desperately with the intro-duction, I took a break. In true Zen fashion, I made myself a nice big mug of tea. In somewhat untrue Zen fashion, I dumped about three tablespoons of sugar in there and then chugged the whole thing. I was just sitting down for Round Two of my battle with the introduction when the caffeine-and-sugar rush hit. Then I was way too fidgety to pore through the whole intro, so I started just flipping my way around the diagrams and pictures. The concept was pretty simple. A Zen garden was a gigantic sandbox with some gravel and maybe three rocks in it — and, often, no plants whatsoever. So really, calling it a "garden" made about as much sense as calling my sandal a "chocolate factory." I guess it was an *ironic* kind of garden. What you did was rake the sand into lines and patterns around the rocks without trying to make any particular picture or shape. If you succeeded in getting yourself into the Zen state of "no-mind" — sort of focused without being focused — your garden would flow naturally and perfectly from your unconscious and you would become one with nature. Also, it would look really pretty.

I had to pee.

Then I needed another mug of tea. The first one had been so sweet and good.

When I got back to the table, I looked under one of the garden pictures and found this quote from the *Book of Tao*: "The Tao which can be spoken of is not the true Tao." I remembered from Houston that Tao had about five different definitions, but basically meant either "true reality" or "the Way." If this meant I couldn't understand the Way of Zen gardening just by reading words, then it was time for some field research. I grabbed a shoebox, cut the sides down until they were only about an inch and a half high, and put on my windbreaker and sandals. Then I ran to the bathroom to pee again. When I finally got out of the apartment, I headed over to the dinky and dilapidated little playground across the street, which had a sandbox. I looked around to make sure nobody was looking, and, sure enough, I was the only idiot out playing in the sandbox in freezing weather. So I scooped up about an inch of sand into my shoebox and jogged back across the street, not much enjoying the feeling of icy sand between my toes. Then I realized my garden wasn't complete yet, and bent down to grab a couple of little stones. This made me spill my sand, so I had to run back to the sandbox and get some more sand. Some old biddy came creaking around the corner of the playground with her walker, saw me, and said, "Excuse me! What do you think you're doing?"

I felt like saying, *A fascinating philosophical query! What do you think I'm doing?* or *I'm stealing sand. Don't you know it's the new craze among people who*

still have teeth nowadays? But that would have pro-
longed the encounter, and I had to get back into
the apartment. And pee some more. So I just said,
"School project," and darted away, trying to balance
my handful of pebbles, my box of sand, and the
needs of my screaming bladder. She shouted after
me, "What ever happened to reading and writing?"
but I was already halfway across the street.

Note to self: It's hard to attain a state of no-mind
when you're incredibly pumped up on tea and sugar
and have to urinate every three and a half minutes.
The Zen garden was kind of intriguing, though. When
my mom got home, she found me raking patterns
in it with four sharpened pencils taped together side
by side. And walking in little circles around the
kitchen and living room. And making the occasional
beeline for the plumbing facilities. When I showed
her what I'd been doing — my garden masterpiece — she looked at me and laughed. "This isn't
like you, San. You're taking the initiative. I don't
think I've ever seen you jump into schoolwork like
this before. Not that I'm complaining, but why the

change?" She cocked her head to one side. "Is this about . . . a girl?"

I paced and snorted, snorted and paced. "Yeah, right. A girl! Like girls are just swarming to scrawny new kids who like to play with sand. Like I'm some irresistible only-minority-kid-in-whiteville superstud. Like —"

"Oh, come on, San! I was just wondering," she said as she walked out of the room to change out of her work clothes. She hated her work clothes, especially those clunky rubber-soled nurse shoes. "Whatever is motivating you, keep it up, OK?"

What's with the "keep it up" thing? Was it, like, the town motto of Harrisonville? I couldn't think about it too hard, because we had a library to visit. I went to put the lid on my garden, and screamed an embarrassingly shrill scream. There was a spider — a brown and hairy spider — upside down inside the lid. I started smacking the lid against the garden in a panic. Any second the spider might skitter around from below and bite my hand. Yikes! My mom came running, but stopped and sighed when she saw the cause of my horror.

"Oh, Sanny, it's only a little house spider. They're friendly. They eat bad bugs."

Great, the fact that they are terrible venomous insect carnivores was very comforting. "Can you kill it, Mom?"

By this time the spider had fallen down into the bottom of the box. Now I had a Zen phobia garden. How special! Mom brushed me aside, shooed the spider onto the second-biggest pebble, and carried the stone, spider and all, out of the apartment, down the stairs, and out onto the scrubby front lawn. I watched in disgusted awe as she wiped the spider gently off the rock and into the grass. Then I went to the bathroom and peed while she climbed back up. When I got back to the table, Mom had put the arachnid-tainted rock back into the garden.

Yuck-o.

With some begging on my part, I finally got her to take the rock back out of the garden and leave it by the front walk on the way to the library. All the way up the block, though, she insisted on blabbing on about how wonderful spiders were, ecologically important, a marvel of biology, blah blah blah. You know, cobras are pest-eating marvels of biology too, but you don't see me rushing to scatter them about the apartment.

I marched my mother right up to the library's information desk and rang the bell. I was in a hurry, very aware of two things: I wanted to get a lot of reading done, and I didn't want to be seen in a public place with my white mom — which would kind of blow my whole "Super-Asian" persona right out of the water, especially if anyone started asking her any questions about our life. There was a rustling in the little back room, and I allowed myself a moment of hope that the lovely Amanda would soon appear. Instead, Mildred came out. She was in a pink sweater with bows over a dark green skirt with tights, which gave her a sort of "grasshopper out on the town" look. She was happy to see me. "Ah, San Lee! I was hoping you'd come back today. Two other students from your school were here already this evening, getting information for your world religions project. . . ."

OH, NO!

"But I knew you had all the good books on Zen in your reserve pile, so I steered them toward Hinduism and Confucianism."

OH, YES! Thank you, Mildred!

My mom thanked Mildred and introduced herself: "Hello, I'm Diane Lee, San's mother. Thank you for helping him out yesterday. I've never seen him so excited about a school project."

"Well, Mr. Dowd works wonders. Every year at this time, children I've never seen before, even though they were born in this town, come stumbling into the library in droves to get cards just for his project."

They smiled at each other for a moment, sharing some secret adult satisfaction of breaking in another generation to the yoke of book slavery. Then, while they filled out the rest of the form for my card, I wandered around a bit. I looked down one aisle and couldn't help noticing that Amanda was reshelving books about twenty feet from me. She saw me, smiled, gestured in a circle, and mouthed one word: "Books!" I started to smile back, but then she ducked down to reach a low shelf and I saw a horrific vision behind her. Peter was walking toward me, with his face buried in what looked like an encyclopedia.

I ducked into the next aisle before he could look up and catch me being a fake, adopted, research-based Buddhist. I sat down on a step stool so I could peek at Amanda and Peter between the shelved books. Peter was talking with her and I could hear some of what she was saying, too: "Popular topic lately . . . I'm not really the expert, but . . ."

She moved down a few feet; Peter followed, and so did I. I grabbed a book out of the shelf between us so I could see and hear better. Glancing at it, I had a shock. It was called *Zen in the Art of Archery*. What were the chances I had wound up in the Zen aisle again? I heard Amanda say, "Lucky boy! You're just one aisle away from what you need."

Geez, she'd called *me* "lucky boy" yesterday. My luck was running out fast. Peter walked by, heading toward my right. I scurried to my left at top speed, and got around the corner before they started up the Zen aisle. I leaned back against the cool gray metal of the shelf edge with a sigh of relief. Just then

I heard my mom's voice calling me. "San! Sanny!" I was thinking, *Shoot me now,* as I scurried back to the info desk before she could get even louder.

Skidding up next to her I said, "Sssssshhhhh! Mom, this is a *library*!"

She was momentarily stunned by my fierce support for library rules, but then snapped back, "Darn, I thought we were in KFC! Guess I can't check out that bucket of extra-crispy, then. Relax, San. Here's your card."

She handed it to me. Wow, my first Pennsylvania library card. And it was still warm from the laminating machine! "Uh, thanks, Ma," I said. "Now let's go!" I took her by the arm and started steering her in the direction of the checkout line. Then Mildred called after us, "Hey, *Zen in the Art of Archery*! I must have missed that one yesterday. It's an oldie but goodie. You're quite the little researcher, San. Mrs. Lee, your boy is pretty quick in the stacks."

I thought, *You have no idea, Mildy baby.* I gave her a little thank-you wave over my shoulder, and we got into the checkout line. I was trying to stare unobtrusively at the ends of the stacks, waiting for Peter to pop out and bust me with the huge stack of Zen books that the checkout lady was loading into my arms. I could feel the cold sweat of fear dripping down the back of my neck as my mom asked the desk lady question after question about our library privileges, the branch's hours, and even where to get a good cappuccino in town on a budget, but we got away clean.

As far as I knew.

We set out, and when we got outside it had started to snow lightly. All the way home, I felt like my arms were about to break off, and my bladder was at its limit, primed to explode like a liquid piñata. My mom asked me if I wanted to stop at a coffee shop around the corner for a bargain cappuccino and I almost died on the spot — I was never going to ingest caffeine again. I smiled weakly and told her I was just too excited about getting back to my research to stop for anything.

Ten grueling minutes later I was in my little room, sitting in the zazen position with the archery book

on my lap. One thing about my new spiritual practices: They helped you if you were too poor to afford
a desk. And this book would help if you were too
poor to afford sleeping pills. It was skinny, but way
hard to read. I got the basic point, though: This
German guy went to a great archery Zen master in
Japan, and studied with him for six years. Then he
wrote the book. What he learned is that in order
to become a true master of anything, you have to
repeat it over and over again with precisely correct
form. Then eventually, if you truly get the form down
to the point where you are totally unconscious of
what you are doing, you will be a master.

Maybe there was some way Woody and I could
repeat something over and over again until we were
Zen masters of it. But what? Sharpening pencils?
Making paper airplanes? Thumb wrestling? And if it
took the archery guy six years to get good at shooting an arrow, I had a weird feeling we might need an
extension on our project deadline.

Or, you know, we could just totally fake it.

NO-MIND

There I was on my special Zen rock, the warm rays of the rising sun bathing me in the happy glow of a new dawn. After twenty minutes of zazen, my butt was numb, sure, but the grass was blanketed with a soft inch of new snow, my homework was done, and the girl of my dreams was striding across the white lawn to greet me. I was at peace. I was in the zone. I was Zen Master San. I was —

COLD! With a huge *THWACK* and then a huge *THWUMP*, an avalanche of snow fell from the overhanging branches of the big tree, covering me from head to bare toes. I almost jumped up and screamed, but caught myself when I realized Woody was watching, her eyes wide. I smiled in false serenity as a chunk of snow ran down the back of my neck and into my shirt collar.

"Oh, San!" Woody said. "The tree —"

"The tree is lighter now. Its branches have given up their burden."

"But your back! And your feet! Aren't you cold?" She started dusting the snow off of me. This was good.

"What is cold? I am having a great morning," I said. Woody kept dusting. I heard footsteps running away from the base of the tree behind me. HEY! Had someone knocked the snow down onto me purposely? Why would anyone do that? I wanted to turn and see who it was, but didn't want to ruin the moment.

When Woody and I had gotten me somewhat plowed-off, I hopped down from my perch — definite progress from the day before, when I had been paralyzed after the first ten minutes. As I landed lightly, with the grace of a slightly damp jungle cat, Woody asked me, "So, did you have any breakthrough ideas for our project last night?"

"Not exactly, but I have two great concepts we could start with. One is compassion, which is a huge component of Zen. The other is 'beginner's mind.'"

"What's that?"

"Basically, it means that experts sometimes defeat themselves by thinking too much. So, those who study a Zen art practice the steps involved over and over again until they can do them without thinking at all. When the actions have become totally instinctive, the student has become a master. 'Beginner's mind' also refers to getting rid of preconceptions and seeing everything as though you're seeing it for the first time." I bent over, scooped up a handful of clean snow, and said, "How many times have you seen snow before? And you'll be like, 'Oh, snow. Whatever,' instead of thinking about what an amazing thing it is. I used to be like that, but then I spent last winter in Texas, where there's no snow." I put a little bit of the snow on my lip and stuck my tongue out to lick it off. "We even forget that snow tastes good." Woody reached out and gently swooped her finger through the snow in my palm; it tickled. She stuck her finger in her mouth and grinned.

"You're right, San — it *is* good!" She bent down and got her own double handful. "There's something else too. Look at the snow in my hand really, really closely. Closer . . . closer . . ."

Our bodies were maybe a foot apart, tops, and my face was so close to her hands that I could feel the cold radiating from the snow to the tip of my nose. I tried to focus my eyes on one individual flake. Woody's eyes were cast down at the snow she was holding too, and she was looking intently at it. Then her eyes lifted to mine, and she held my gaze for what felt like a whole minute as electric waves shot through my whole body. Was Woody going to kiss me? Right here, three days after I met her, at 7:30 in the morning, twenty steps from the bus line?

The corners of her eyes crinkled up in merriment, and she leaned in even closer. Then she BLEW on the snow, sending a little shower up into my face. She laughed as I wiped my eyes on the scratchy plastic sleeve of my windbreaker. Then I laughed too. I grabbed a handful of snow and flung it at her. She ducked, but I got her hair a little. She made a snow-ball and flung it at my back. We wound up having a pretty fierce little mini snowball fight. Then we heard the late bell ring. We looked around and noticed everyone but us had already gone inside. She gave me the "uh-oh" look, and we grabbed up our book bags and her guitar. We started giggling, and couldn't stop all the way into school. The secretary who gave us our late passes asked for a reason, and Woody said, "Avalanche." We left the office together, and laughed our way to our lockers.

Woody's homeroom was just down the hall from mine, so I kind of dropped her off there. How slick was that? I had just walked a girl to class! We did the "Uh, see ya," "Um, okay," thing for maybe thirty seconds, until her homeroom teacher broke it up by saying, "Miss Long, would you like to join us today?" I strutted away down the hall, flying high. In first period, I hummed my way into my English room, and found the teacher handing out copies of a paperback book with laminated covers. It was called *The Tao of Pooh*. Oh, geez! It was a book about Asian philosophy. It looked like we were going to do one of those units where the English teacher and the social studies teacher work together. Don't they know kids hate that? It's creepy to think of the teachers conspiring with each other. Plus, this was going to ratchet up the Zen pressure; I would have to fool a whole 'nother class. And a whole 'nother teacher.

Yikes!

The day got stranger too. In gym, we were doing basketball. I was alone, shooting baskets at this one hoop in the corner that didn't even have a net; everyone else was either playing three-on-three or watching a game that was going on between three jock guys and three of the gym teachers. The gym teachers were slaying the jocks. Not that I cared.

Even though Peter Jones was one of the jocks involved. And Woody was watching the game. And I was watching Woody. She looked beautiful, even in our school's dorky brown gym shorts and a Harrisonville Hawks T-shirt. Most of the girls looked kind of clumpy and pale, but Woody was elegant somehow. She just always held her head a little higher than anybody else.

Not that I noticed. I was Zen Hoop Boy. I decided to test out the whole repeat-the-steps-until-your-no-mind-takes-over thing with foul shots. This was a good test, because even though I'm pretty tall, I've never been much of a shooter. I concentrated on keeping my breathing even and my feet planted just behind the line. I put my left hand on the side of the ball for stability, bent my knees, pushed with my right hand and straightened my legs with one smooth motion. The shot missed by a mile, and my right sandal flopped off on the follow-through. As I was retrieving the ball, I may or may not have stopped to check out Woody's legs, but that didn't interfere with my laserlike concentration.

Right.

I took fifteen or so more shots, remembering that the Zen archery guys never cared about whether their arrows hit the target as long as the form was right. There was this famous story I'd read about a Zen master archer who was in a target-shooting contest with, like, a hundred monks at a Zen monastery on a cliff overlooking the Pacific Ocean in California. The other guys shot all of their rounds, and this great master guy was supposed to shoot last. When it was his turn, he drew an arrow, strung it up on his bow, and, in one smooth motion, shot it straight over the cliff edge and into the sea. When it hit, he said, "Bull's-eye!" And everyone agreed he was the champion.

Judging from the shots I'd just taken, he was *my* kind of champion.

After just one more tiny peek at Woody, who was still watching the game, I stopped trying to tune out the gym noise and let it wash over me instead. I stopped trying to ignore the flatness and bald tread of the ball I was using. I even gave myself over to the slightly funky and mildew-enhanced odor of the gym, which was flavored with the sharpness of sweaty rubber. And I stopped counting my shots. Dribble, set, shoot. Dribble, set, shoot. Dribble . . . set . . . shoot. The sound of the warning bell snapped me out of my trance, and I looked around. The young-jock-versus-aging-jock Olympiad had ended without me noticing, but a glance at the scoreboard got me up to speed: Peter and company had gotten demolished.

That was worth a half smile.

And Woody was behind me, the last girl out of the gym, leaning on the closed-up bleachers and watching my devastating exhibition of no-mind skill. Her perfect ruby lips opened and she said, "Hey, San. Keep that up and you'll get one in someday soon."

I looked at her in sudden, abject despair. She smiled, strode over, grabbed the ball from me, and elbowed me aside. Then she drained five straight. I could have cried, but it felt great to be with her, alone, for the second time in one day. She said, "Let me see you shoot again," and bounce-passed the ball to me. Perfectly.

I did, and missed. Four times. My ears were getting red. My cheeks were getting red. Who am I kidding? My *everything* was getting red. "One more," Woody ordered. But this time, as I bent my knees, she reached around from behind me with both hands to correct my arm positioning. I still missed, but her body was pressed to mine as we followed through together. *Bull's-eye,* I thought. Then the late bell rang.

the wednesday
plan

The week went on, with a boring weekend of Zen reading in there somewhere. Woody visited me every schoolday morning at my rock — sometimes with Peter, sometimes without. She sang "Hard Travelin'" at lunch, looking into my eyes. It was a good song. We brainstormed and rejected ideas in social studies every day: Writing haiku was perfect, writing haiku was boring; making tea for the class was cool, making a stimulant for a bunch of eighth graders was a no-no; Zen basketball was brilliant, if Zen basketball was so brilliant, why was I still shooting three for ten from the free-throw line?

Then on Tuesday, I brought in my Zen garden to see what Woody would think. The groups were spread out all over the room, and we grabbed a nice table in a pool of sun by the window. She loved messing around with the four-pencil rake. I loved being close together, and watching the lines of her thoughts tracing their way between the stones. She did the whole thing playfully, which was exactly perfect. I always stopped to think about making my lines straight, or making the whole image in the garden look relaxing, or whatever. But Woody just raked and giggled.

When she had the garden right — and you could definitely tell, somehow, that it was right — she handed me the rake. My hand was sweaty, but I could tell when I held the pencils that hers wasn't. Before sliding the garden over to me, she put the lid on and shook it. I opened the lid back up, and she said, "Look! No garden!" Which was perfect too.

I bent to my work, and smelled Woody's shampoo — something orangey. I felt the warmth of the sun on the backs of my hands. Closing my eyes, I dropped the rocks randomly over the sand. I looked, nudged one over about half an inch to the left, and started raking my lines. I wanted to look cool for Woody, so I was working on a show of nonchalance — which I know is an oxymoron. She smiled; I smiled. We were having a moment! Then, just when I had the garden complete, a strong gust of frigid air blew my sand everywhere. I looked up, and there was Peter — who had just opened the window wide.

I could have sworn I saw a look of triumph flash across his face before he made eye contact with me. "Oh, San, I'm so sorry. I didn't see your — uh — sandbox there. Did I ruin your work?"

I thought fast, then grinned. "Thank you, Peter. Thank you for teaching me the lesson of imper-manence."

Heh-heh. Woody and I had another moment. And whether he was standing three feet away or not, Peter wasn't invited.

After Peter walked away muttering, I noticed that Dowd was looking at me kind of funny. Oh, well. I had some sand to clean up. Woody and I tried scoop-ing the sand with the box lid, which worked for a while. When we got down to the fine stuff, though, we had to switch to using the edge of a piece of paper. Woody went up to Dowd's desk to grab a piece of masking tape so she could get the sand off her sweater. I grabbed Woody's project assignment sheet, and flipped it over so I could make a crease down the middle for pouring. On the back side, Woody had drawn a whole bunch of red hearts with the capital letters "ELL" in all of them.

There went the freakin' moment. Who was this ELL person? What kind of stupid initials were ELL anyway? I looked around out of the corner of my eye as I scooped, but there was nobody in the class with a last name that started with "L" — just me and Woody. I glanced at Peter, who was back with his partner, Abby. She was building what looked like a scale model of the Taj Mahal out of those perforated craft sticks social studies teachers love — a pretty impressive model, by the way — while Peter was breaking the sticks as she needed them. I was pleased to note that it looked like he was snapping them with more force than was strictly required by the physics of the situation. But Peter was suddenly unimportant; his initials were P-something-J.

Of course, Woody had other classes in her schedule besides social studies. Maybe this guy was smoothly moving in on her during her first period math class while I was innocently studying English right down the hall. Or maybe he didn't even go to our school. Maybe he was some disgusting high school pervert who couldn't get a girl his own age. Oh, God. There were probably tons of high school guys calling Woody at all hours, and I didn't even have her phone number. What chance did I have with a girl as cool as Woody anyway? Just because I was her flavor of the week right now, that didn't mean we were, like, destined to be soul mates. Maybe she liked me as a friend because I had fooled her into thinking we shared some interests, or maybe she was just stringing me along until our project was due. And I had fallen for it!

Well, I wasn't going to just stand by and let this ELL make a fool of me! I wasn't just going to lie down and surrender the girl of my dreams to some pimply, hairy freshman guy! I would fight back! I would take Woody in my arms and —

Oh, who was I kidding? I would quit, that's what I'd do. There were plenty of other beautiful, smart, talented girls with excellent foul-shooting skills who would just love to date an authentic, honest, down-to-earth guy like me. Who happened to be a pretend Zen master.

Woody came back with a big ball of tape rolled around her fist, and started brushing her sweater down with it. As she reached up to get a dusting of sand off her shoulder, she noticed the writing on my paper scoop, and tried to snatch it out of my hand. But that made her tape ball catch on her hair.

"Oww!" she cried. Good! What did I care? I was a pretend Zen master. I had no earthly attachments or desires, at least in theory. The Four Noble Truths were right — attachment to desire really sucked.

Woody looked at me. "Can you help me get this untangled, San? I'm stuck."

I laid the paper down and reached up in a cool and unattached way to separate her hair, strand by strand, from the tape ball. The orange scent enveloped me, and her hair was soft and lovely in my hands. Fortunately I was beyond noticing all that, and had been for a good twenty seconds already.

When we were all sorted out again, Woody went back to getting the last bits of sand off her sweater while I did NOT watch. Then she gently picked the incriminating paper out of my hand, said, "I'll just throw this out now," and walked over to the garbage can. While I did NOT watch.

She looked at the paper one more time before she chucked it, and when she came back to our work desk, she was blushing a little. I tried to pretend nothing had happened, which was hard because this girl had a pull on me that would probably have overwhelmed a man of lesser meditation talents. And she plunged into packing up her stuff and copying down the homework as though nothing had happened.

But the scent of orange lingered on my hands for hours.

That night, lying in bed, I realized my dad was going to be calling again after school the next day. I'd pick up the phone, and the prison operator would ask me to accept a collect call from Texas. I'd say yes, knowing that the call would cost us money that my mom didn't have, money that should have been spent paying down my dad's legal bills or our credit card debt. I could hear his smooth voice saying, *I missed talking with you last week, buddy. Now tell me everything!* So I'd start telling him everything, but I wouldn't really. I'd only tell him what he wanted to hear: I was fitting in, my grades were good, I was helping my mother in this "difficult time." Somewhere in the middle, he'd interrupt to tell me his whitewashed story: He was innocent, he was framed, I had to believe in him and everything would be fine in the end.

He was a top-grade liar, and I was his top-grade liar son.

I couldn't do it. I couldn't pretend I believed him, or that I didn't hate every molecule of his vile, manipulative soul, or that everything would be fine. It was bad enough that my mom fell for all his crap. And for all of my crap. Lying to the king liar was somehow the worst thing of all.

So I started looking for an angle: something that would keep me away on Wednesday afternoons, preferably for months on end. Until my dad got the hint and stopped calling. I could get in trouble every Tuesday so I'd have detention every Wednesday — but that wouldn't go with my Zen image. I could join a sports team that practiced on Wednesdays — except for the whole "San sucks at sports" issue. I could jump off a moderately high cliff every Tuesday so I'd be in the hospital every Wednesday. But with my luck, my mom would be my nurse and my dad would get special permission to fly to Pennsylvania and visit me. Just what I needed: tons of medical bills, my mom having an excuse to stick me full of needles, and my father chained to my bedside between two armed marshals.

So that plan wouldn't work.

I needed something that wasn't painful, that played to my strengths, that kept me out of trouble with my mom. Wait! Something that *played to my strengths*! I HAD IT! I sat bolt upright in bed, banging my head resoundingly on my cheap overhanging reading lamp. But physical pain no longer mattered to me; I was a Zen man with a Zen plan.

A plan with no downside.

wash your bowl

On my rock the next morning, I achieved a moment of near-perfect insight. I mean, I know I was only fake meditating, but come on — don't cubic zirconiums sparkle too? For once, I forgot about my breathing. I forgot about forgetting about my breathing. I forgot about my dad, and telephones, and avoiding my dad and telephones. Hot and cold, money and no money, Woody and ELL sitting in a tree, it was all one. And all not one.

If someone had handed me a basketball then, I could have sunk ten straight, nothing but net. The sun was upon me, the clean wind was around me, and the air smelled of fresh snow and . . . oranges?

The next thing I knew, I was on my back. Woody was jumping around over me, laughing, rubbing her hands together to remove the small amount of snow she *hadn't* smushed into my eyes from behind. I wiped my face and smiled up at her. She was wearing a cable-knit sweater and jeans. No gloves, sneakers with no socks. And those purple glasses. Her cheeks were flushed with the cold, and her hair was blowing around her face. She was beautiful.

I mean, if earthly desires are your kind of thing.

"Good morning, Woody. Thanks for the wake-up."

"The pleasure was all mine. Now, guess what? I have it!"

"Have what?" I asked as I propped myself on my elbows.

"The project, silly! I'll teach you how to shoot foul shots — Zen hoops! That's what you were doing in gym the other day, right? The beginner's-mind thing you told me about? Dowd used to coach the basketball team. He'll love it! Plus, I know a ton about basketball, because my father spent my whole childhood trying to turn me into a boy. Might as well make it work for us, right?"

"Hmm, well, that's definitely a plan. But I have an idea too. Can you come somewhere with me after school today?"

"Where? For what?"

"The soup kitchen. I was thinking, since we sort of

planned to go there together anyway, why not use it as our project? You know, because of the compassion concept. We could start today, I bet."

"But doesn't that seem kind of unfair, San? Like if we were planning to do it anyway, we're not really showing any extra compassion. We're just using the poor people to help us get a grade."

Which was so untrue. I was also using them to avoid showing respect to my parent, and get a cheap date. "Well, I thought about that, Woody. But then I thought, how can feeding people be immoral? Right action is right action."

"Is that, like, a Zen saying?"

"Yes, it is *a lot* like a Zen saying!"

She sighed. "OK, San. How about this? We'll do both: the basketball and the soup kitchen. Then we'll definitely get an A. Unless you're getting too sick of me already? Peter says I sometimes come on too strong and . . ."

Grrr. What was with Peter anyway? All I knew was that he and Woody sometimes got a ride together, that he had a great right jab, and that his initials weren't

ELL. "No, that's fine. I mean, it's okay. It's great, I mean. It's excellent. But I am really bad at basketball."

"I know. I saw!"

"So, what if I don't impro —"

"You will, San. You will. Just give yourself over to me. And to, you know, the Force or whatever."

"Uh, Woody, the Force isn't actually a Zen concept."

"Yeah, I know. That was a joke. In case *give yourself over to me* sounded too, um, intense or anything."

"No, it didn't sound intense." I took a deep breath and released it slowly. Here was the big question: "Uh, should it have?"

She looked away as she spoke. "Did you want it to?"

Good God. This could go on forever, or until I had a heart attack. Plus, we were going to be late again, and Woody's heart was pledged to ELL anyway — so what was the use? "I try not to cultivate . . . uh . . . earthly attachments. Buddha said that releasing one's attachments is the key to attaining peace and enlightenment."

Woody turned her head sharply so that she was facing even farther away from me, and I heard an artificial-sounding laugh. "Right, of course. Let's go, San. We're going to be late." As I got up off the rock, she looked back at me. "San, there's some snow in your hair." She wiped it off with the backs of her fingers, then pulled them away like my eyebrows were on fire. And truthfully, I felt like they kinda were.

With weird unstated vibes floating all around, we trudged into school. And we were late anyway. I swear, if I ever write a book, I'm going to call it *Zen in the Art of Almost Picking Up Girls, Then Blowing It Forever for No Good Reason.*

I walked with Woody to her homeroom, but we weren't really together — just two people walking parallel to each other down an ugly green hallway. She did give me a little wave when we got to her locker, and I did give her a little wave back, but it wasn't like things had been back in the glory days of our relationship, fifteen minutes before.

You know those stupid triangle football things that sixth graders make out of aluminum foil so they can flick them across the lunch table? There was one of those on the floor in the hallway, and I kicked it over and over again, all the way to my locker. I'm lucky I didn't cut my toe — sandals aren't the traditional footwear of placekickers — but it felt good to just kick something really hard.

I opened my locker, which was a very Zen locker: nothing in it but three textbooks, all neatly covered. I'm not actually neat, but not owning anything has a way of uncluttering a kid's life. I hung my Astros jacket and pulled out the books. As I did, a note fell off of the top book; someone must have shoved it through the little vent slots in the locker door. It was folded over in fourths and typed on a piece of thick, expensive stationery, like the paper my dad had always used to print résumés on every time we moved. The font was one of those angular-looking fake-Asian ones:

THE PURPOSE OF ZEN IS THE PERFECTION OF CHARACTER.

— YAMADA ROSHI

Well, that was cryptic. And it was the very same quote I had used in my English journal. How did someone know that and why did they want to throw it back in my face? I had no time to think about it too hard. There was only about a minute left in homeroom, and I needed to skim the first chapter of *The Tao of Pooh* really, really fast. Or, you know, check out the homeroom chicks and babes, now that Woody had ELL and I had no earthly attachments. There was this one girl named Stephanie who was pretty cute. She was tiny and red-haired, nothing like . . . well, nothing like some other girls I knew. And then there was this girl named Keisha, who had kind of a sophisticated hip-hop look going on. And she was really smart. But I bet she couldn't throw a snowball like . . . She-Who-Must-Not-Be-Named. And over by the textbook shelves, there was Jenna, the official "it" girl of eighth grade. But I wasn't into the "it" girl type. I was into the "smells like oranges" type.

Like I always say, homeroom sucks. And then the bell rings.

I got through most of the day fine, though. Lunch was even OK; Woody played her guitar the whole time, so I didn't have to face her. Then, in social studies, we didn't meet with our partners. Instead, Dowd gave a lecture on how religious traditions get passed down. He happened to mention that when Zen Buddhism first came to China, there were six successive leaders. The first guy, Bodhidharma, picked his replacement, who in turn picked *his* replacement, et cetera. Dowd said they were kind of like popes, except that the system broke down after the sixth guy, and Zen split into several different schools.

Big whoop, right? But as it turns out, you never notice the really important stuff until it comes back to bite you later.

When school let out, Woody sent Peter on his way, and then waited for me at the classroom door. "So," she asked while staring at the gum on somebody's locker, "are we going to the shelter and volunteering?"

"Yeah, I guess so," I told my sandals. "If you're up for it."

"I'm up for it," Woody announced to the ceiling tiles.

"Excellent," I exclaimed to the antidrug poster on Dowd's door. "Let's go."

We went.

The shelter was about half a mile from the school, across several big streets with traffic lights, so we had a good, solid fifteen-minute walk together. We talked about homework (we were both against it), and teachers (we both thought they were strange alien beings that couldn't be trusted, although she thought Dowd was "interesting, at least"). But we stayed on the safe topics — nothing about our real lives, nothing about our real feelings.

Nothing about earthly attachments.

And then it was compassion time. We got to this old and decrepit-looking building with a line of maybe twenty-five people waiting in front. In the cold and the slush. Some of them looked like I'd expect people waiting in line for a soup kitchen meal to look: dirty, scraggly, old, pushing shopping carts full of blankets and random junk. But others looked like regular working people. And there were two mothers there with little kids. Somehow it had never occurred to me that there might be little kids lining up in the snow for a meal, in America in the twenty-first century.

What were they thinking as they saw all the other pedestrians walking in a wide arc to avoid coming anywhere near the line, like being poor was contagious?

Woody pulled me past the spectacle, around the corner of the building, and into a side door. As soon as we were inside the shelter, an elderly woman came scurrying up to Woody. "Emily, dear, it's wonderful to see you. And I see you've brought a friend. Are you bringing in your donation for the month?"

Emily? Who the heck was —

"No, Sister Mary Clare. I'm here with my friend San Lee to volunteer. We want to help out with serving. Um, it's for a school project. Can we?"

Sister Mary Clare looked me up and down. "Well, he's not much in the wardrobe department, but then again, neither was our Lord and Savior. Can you wash dishes, Stanley?"

"Um, it's San Lee."

"Right, Stanley. That's what I said."

"No, I —"

Emily, the artist formerly known as Woody, stomped on my foot and cut me off. "Yes, San is an excellent dishwasher. He's quick and thorough. The trick is, you can't get too attached to any one dish — you just have to keep moving on to the next dish with no emotion. And that's San's specialty."

Ouch. Easy for Mrs. ELL to talk about how other people moved from dish to dish. I didn't have time to respond, though, because at that very instant Mildred Romberger came barreling out of a door marked PANTRY holding a wedge of cheese. "See?" she cackled. "*You're* the senile one, Mary Clare! Here's the Parmesan cheese you said we didn't have. Now we can make great garlic cheese bread with the butter you *also* said we didn't have. Oh, hello, San. How's my favorite Zen student today?"

What was this, the Soup Kitchen of the Ancients? And was Mildred going to blow my cover? I had to change the topic. "I'm doing great, thank you. I'm here to wash dishes. But I'm wondering . . . umm . . . no offense, but aren't there any . . . uh . . . younger people helping out here?"

Sister Mary Clare answered that one: "Well, Stanley, far too many young people seem to be too busy to think about others. Not like your friend Emily here. When she came to me last year with her first donation, I thought, 'This will never happen again; she's just another little rich girl making herself feel good.' Then she showed up again a month later, and a month after that, and so on — thirteen months and counting. Our Emily is a rare girl. So, are the two of you an item, Stan? If so, we'll try not to leave you alone together in the dishwashing area for too long! Right, Mildred?"

Then the two oldsters started cackling together uproariously. Oh, good lord. Or jumping Buddhas. This might have been the first recorded instance of a nun and a librarian trying to set a fake Buddhist up with a dentist's folksinger daughter for a hot soup-kitchen dishwashing rendezvous. Too bad they didn't know that "Emily's" heart was already pledged to the mysterious ELL. Or that I was famous for my emotional detachment and lack of earthly desires. All that was going to happen in the dishwashing room was the cleaning of dishes.

Darn it.

Sister Mary Clare gave us a quick tour of the dining room, pantry, and main kitchen area. Then she hustled us into the back of the kitchen, gave us aprons and rubber gloves, and taught us how to be dishwashers. First, these huge trays came through a little window in front of us on a conveyor belt. Then we'd stop the belt when a tray was over the huge sink, grab a handheld showerhead-type thing, and blast the dishes on the tray with the superhot water from the shower to rinse them. Next, we'd start the conveyor again, maneuver the tray into this stainless-steel box, and pull the WASH lever, which would start a five-minute cycle to get the dishes really clean. Finally we'd yank the lever back up, wait for a green light on the side of the box, turn the conveyor back on again, and shove the next tray into place.

It sounded easy, but that was before the action started. The trays were coming in maybe three at a time, and they were completely piled up with disgusting gooey dishes, plates, bowls, and silverware. But the silverware was supposed to be separate, so then one of us would have to reach in amid the tottering, muck-crusted piles on the moving tray and pluck it out. Also, you couldn't put napkins through the machine, so we'd have to check for those too. And if you've never tried to separate a soda-drenched napkin from a moving bowl of half-eaten chocolate pudding without causing a dish avalanche, you haven't really lived.

Plus the shower water was like a hundred-and-fifty degrees, and it splattered all over you if it bounced off a dish at the wrong angle. And you were constantly bouncing water off at the wrong angle, because you kept looking at your dishwashing partner:

— Was she looking at you?

— Darn it! She kind of was. Did she just catch you looking at her?

— Why was she trying to catch you looking at her anyway? Shouldn't she be concentrating on the dishes? Or on her stupid three-initials boyfriend? Or on —

OWW! That water really was off the *hizzook* hot.

By the end of the three-hour dinner shift, we were totally soaked, and totally covered with grunge, and it was about ninety-five degrees in the dish room. We hadn't seen a single guest (that's what they called the people who came to eat) since we'd come in, but we'd seen enough plates to know that dinner had been a hit. And as the last tray rolled out of the washer, we were tired. Or at least I was. My arms were shaky from the unusual strain of slinging the trays and the hose around, my neck was stiff, and my feet hurt like a madman.

Mildred stuck her head into our little window and said, "That's it, kids! You can relax now." I took off my apron, threw it on the steaming pile of used dishrags, and hopped up to sit on the steel counter. As I flicked a strand of half-washed spaghetti off of my pant leg, Woody jumped up next to me. I waited for her to say something. She waited too. Just when the waiting was starting to feel like some strange Zen duel, Sister Mary Clare popped in with two plates of food.

"Here you go, kids! You did a great job of keeping up for first-timers. Why, I remember once in 1978, the chief of police lost a bet to Mildred and had to wash the dishes here for a week. On his first night, the trays were backed up five deep, and then his pistol got stuck in the conveyor and went through the pressure-wash unit. We were all diving to the floor — I thought the heat would make his bullets shoot all over the place! Oh, was *that* a wild time!" She nodded happily. "Yes, a wild time. Anyway, we kept some food warm for you."

I hadn't thought about it, but I was starving. It was going on seven o'clock, and I hadn't eaten a thing since lunch — which, for me, was like a miracle and a half. Woody and I both dived into the food like we'd just spent eleven years as island castaways, and didn't come up for air until the last crumb was a fading memory. Then we started back in with the waiting contest until Mildred barged in.

"Aha!" she crowed. "What are you two youngsters still doing here, all alone together? In a church building, no less. And don't tell me you're just eating either. Your plates are empty, and I'm no fool. I know what it means when two young people look at each other like that!"

Strangely, we had been avoiding looking at each

other for hours. But when she said that, of course, we both looked. I could feel the heat in my face, even above the general swelter of the dish room, as I turned back toward Mildred. "Uh, Mrs. Romberger? Now that we're done eating, what are we supposed to do next?"

She looked absolutely jolly. "You should know this one, Zen Boy: Wash your bowl!"

I did, while Woody left the room for a minute or two. So I washed her bowl too. Although I must have missed a footnote in a book somewhere, because I didn't know what washing bowls had to do with Zen.

Woody came back in, and gave me the no-look look we'd been developing. "Uh, San, this was . . . umm . . . good. I mean, I'm glad we did it."

I no-looked right back at her. "Yeah, uh, me too. And, uh, I washed your bowl too. You know, it's a Zen practice."

She looked puzzled. "What does washing a bowl have to do with Zen?"

"I'll tell you tomorrow, when we have more time. Right now, I have to get home fast."

"Oh, I just called my mom on my cell. Do you want a ride?"

I couldn't accept a ride from Woody's mom. Then Woody might see my mother or something. But then again, I couldn't say no gracefully either. Plus, it was cold and dark out, and I was wearing wet clothes and sandals.

I hesitated too long thinking about all this, and Woody started angrily yanking her coat on. "Yes," I blurted. "I'd love a ride."

As she walked out of the dish room and down the hall, her voice floated behind: "OK, San — if you don't think it's too much of an earthly attachment or anything."

Woody walked right over to a really expensive-looking car that was idling by the curb. She got in the backseat first, and as I slipped in next to her, I felt really awkward. I was sweating and dripping all over the leather seats, and probably smelled like a barn-yard animal — if barnyard animals were ever allowed to roll around in troughs of Parmesan cheese. But the driver had great manners. Either that, or she enjoyed the smell of livestock and sharp cheese.

"Hi, Mom!" Woody chirped. Ah, they were a fake-cheerful family.

"Hi, Emily," the mom replied as she pulled away from the curb. "And you must be San. We've heard so much about you this week: 'San said this. San said that. San sits on a rock.' San, San, San. Truthfully, I think Emily's father and Peter are getting pretty sick of hearing it. No offense. But I think it's great that Emily is being exposed to such . . . diversity. We don't get much chance to meet, um, people like you in our little town."

Woody looked like she wanted to open her door and roll out onto the street, preferably into the path of an oncoming tractor trailer. I wasn't offended by Mrs. Long's awkward little salute to diversity; I was trying to make sense of the Peter thing.

"Peter?" I asked, rather intelligently.

"You know, Peter — from your school. Emily's brother."

"Brother?" Wow, this woman was going to think all Chinese people talked like cavemen.

"Well, stepbrother. When I married Emily's father, we each brought a child along. And now we're one big happy family."

I could have sworn that, even over the road noise and the blast of the heater, I could hear Woody snort. I ignored it and gave Mrs. Long directions to our apartment. When we got there, I thanked her, hopped out, and scrambled for the front door just in case my mom might be in the vicinity.

But I shouldn't have worried about that. Mom was sitting upstairs in the dark, waiting to kill me.

calls and
misses

I walked up the stairs and into the apartment, feeling the ache in muscles I hadn't even known I had. My backpack felt like it weighed 300 pounds, and the soles of my sandals felt like wet sandpaper beneath my feet. This had been a weird day, and a day full of questions: Who put the Zen note in my locker? Why? Why did Woody have two names? Who was ELL? If Peter was Woody's stepbrother, why did he have a thing against me?

Would I smell like Parmesan cheese forever?

I opened the door with a sigh, feeling like a cross between the Hardy Boys and a galley slave. And there, sitting on the tacky rented recliner chair with a glass of wine, was my mom. The lights were all off, except for the dim little lamp over her chair. She sat in the little cone of yellow, like a police interrogator on TV. And from the look on her face, she wasn't playing the good cop.

Before the door could even click shut behind me,

she started in. "Where were you, San? Where WERE you? I called your school, but it was already closed. I was going to call the police if you didn't get home soon. And you missed your father's call — again! Did you know he has to work extra hours shoveling sand and picking up garbage on the edge of the interstate just to earn the right to call? Do you care?"

She stopped to take a sip of wine, and in the faint half-light it looked like a tear was running down her right cheek. She looked at me and waited for the answer that would explain this all away.

"Mom, I'm sorry I kept you waiting. I went to this soup kitchen with a girl in my social studies class — for our project, you know? The Zen thing? Anyway, they kept us washing dishes nonstop, so I couldn't call. I didn't mention this to you? I thought I'd told you —"

WHAP! That was the sound of my mom's hand smacking me across the face. She had never, ever hit me before. I couldn't believe what had happened, so I just stood there, watching the wine from her over-turned glass spill onto the carpet in slow motion.

"Great," she said. "Now the rug is ruined too."

Then she started sobbing. I didn't know what to do in this situation: When someone slaps you and then cries, are you obligated to hug them? Do you ask what's wrong while defending your rib cage at the same time? Do you walk away? Clean up the spreading wine stain?

Stand there like an idiot?

Well, that last one was my choice. I just stood there, feeling the tears welling up in my eyes and the heat rushing to what must have been a bright scarlet handprint on my face. It took my mom about a minute to get herself back under control. Finally she went to the kitchen counter, grabbed a tissue, and blew her nose. Then she said, "I will not have you lying to me, San. I've been lied to enough for this lifetime. You know you did NOT tell me anything about missing your father's call. I am ashamed of you. And you are grounded."

I was going to ask for how long, but I wanted to get out of there with my teeth intact. Instead, I just said, "I won't talk to him." Then I stopped to clear a sudden lump in my throat and blink the moisture out of my eyes before continuing shakily, "I don't care if I'm grounded until I'm a hundred, I won't talk to him."

She didn't look mad anymore, or even particularly sad. Just drained and kind of old. Defeated. "Oh, San," she whispered. "I'm so sorry."

My cheek hurt. I didn't want to hear it. I said, "Whatever. Good night." Then I skulked away into my room, and closed the door. As I looked in the chipped mirror on the back of my door at my face — which looked exactly like it felt — I realized I had just doomed myself to stay in my room until bedtime. Which was hours away.

Looking around, I really felt like a Zen monk. I was in this little battleship-gray room, with no pictures on the walls, no furniture except the bed and a crummy old dresser that tilted to the left, and no electronic devices whatsoever. My dad probably had better access to TV and music than I did. All I had was the pile of books by the bed. And a whole lot of time.

They say, "Everything will look better in the morning." They're pretty much full of crap, though. For one moment as I woke up in a little pool of sunlight, as well as a little pool of drool atop the library book under my head, I thought, *Hey, this is a beautiful day.* Then I realized I was living a life of total deception, in total poverty, among total strangers. With a mom who was probably losing it.

Stalked via stationery, two-timed by a girl with two names. Grounded and slapped.

Oh, well. I still had my health. As I eased my way out of bed and onto the icy linoleum floor, I realized I didn't quite have all of my health. I was incredibly sore all over, and the inside of my cheek was killing me. Apparently, I had bitten it in the process of getting smacked upside the head by my mom. I was almost afraid to look in the mirror, but you couldn't actually see any damage on the outside. At least I could go to school and pretend everything was Zen-normal. Oh, joy.

Have you ever attempted to drown your sorrows in sugared cereal? I have, often. I can't believe we've gotten this far without me mentioning it, but I am probably a Cap'n Crunch addict. In fact, when I was in first grade, this nutrition-expert lady came to our class to teach us about healthy food and asked us to write down our favorite fruits on this little coloring work sheet. I raised my hand and asked, "How do you spell 'Crunch Berries'?"

Anyhow, this was definitely a "date with the Cap'n" kind of morning. I got the milk, a bowl, a cheap-o spoon that my mom had bought in the dollar store, and the economy-sized cereal box, and set up my feasting station. But just as the first jet of cool and delicious milk hit the golden top of my crunch mountain, Mom walked in. She looked like she'd been run over by the Bum Truck — her hair was stringy, she was still in her bathrobe, her face was the color of congealed oatmeal, with reddish splotches on her nose and chin, and purplish bags under her eyes.

As though hitting me had beaten *her* up.

She puttered around with her coffee things while I tried to enjoy digging into my sugar fortification rations. But somehow, having the wreck of your mom pacing back and forth around you in stony silence stomps on the sugar buzz. When she finally sat down across from me, she took a sip of coffee, grimaced, and sighed. Then she spoke.

"Look, San, I've never hit you before. I couldn't sleep all night thinking about it. You're my baby boy. You're all I have, you're the one thing I've got to show for my first thirty-nine years of life. You're the only person I'm sure of. And then when *you* lied to me . . ."

Her eyes were starting to run over. "San, when you started making up some story last night . . . I know you're not genetically related to him, but for a second, you looked just like your father. I'm sorry, but you looked just like your father."

She was weeping freely, and suddenly I was bawling too. If I had ever been itching to try out the intriguing taste of Cap'n Crunch with Tear-Berries, this would have been my chance. Mom came around the table and put her arms around me, which gave me all the excuse I needed to collapse into her. We stayed like that until the cereal was even more of a soggy paste, and then finally got under control again. Mom got up to reheat her cold coffee, and I wiped my nose all over my sleeve while her head was turned.

As she sat back down, I said, "I still can't believe you hit me, Mom."

She said, "I know. I don't think I was really even so mad at you. I really wanted to hit your father."

"Well, Mom, you missed."

She winced, and took a sip of her nuked coffee.

"By the way, I truly was feeding people at the soup kitchen last night."

She gave me the "And?" look.

"And I kind of promised my partner that we could do it every Wednesday. So I know you grounded me, but —"

"Sanny, you can't avoid talking to your father forever."

I just looked at her.

"But," she continued, "if you need some time, I'll run interference with him for a while until you get things figured out."

It was my turn to give her the "And?" look.

"You're still grounded, because you disappeared and scared me to death and lied to me about it when you got home."

I started to argue, but hadn't even managed to get my mouth open when she said, "On the other hand, this girl seems to be a good influence on you. Sooooo . . . I suppose you can go to the soup kitchen on Wednesdays . . ."

I felt like jumping for joy right there in front of my mom and the beaming face of the Cap'n on the side of the box, until she added, "As long as you promise I'll get to meet your little partner sometime soon."

You know, as I got up to put on a different, non-snotted shirt for school, I could almost have sworn I detected some mockery in the Cap'n's expression. It's pretty sad when even two-dimensional, three-fingered pretend admirals are laughing at you.

Like anyone with that goofy freakin' gigundo white mustache had room to talk. Sheesh.

Gym class, five hours later. Woody is putting me to work. She hasn't said anything about the night before, or about my being late to school. Neither have I. She's just watching me take free throws again, standing behind me and a little bit to my left, kicking my feet apart every time she thinks they're too close together. My hands are clammy and I'm feeling all the tight muscles left over from my dishwashing adventure. Plus I'm trying not to think about the whole thing with my mom. But I'm shooting. What else can I do? It's our project.

I shoot and miss, shoot and miss. My toes are cold. I imagine how great it would feel to be wearing a nice pair of thick, warm hightops. But no, I'm wearing my Air Zens, and my feet are suffering accordingly. I hope Woody is at least admiring how stylishly my Harrisonville gym clothes hang on me, because the only set they had left is about three sizes too big for my chickenlike frame. It's a miracle the shorts are staying up at all, and I can feel them drooping to ever-lower levels with every shot. My undies are probably flapping in the breeze for all to see. I can't exactly stop and check, but I'm pretty sure I'm sporting my old-school L.A. Kings boxers.

Yo, check it: I'm the Buddha Gangsta.

Just when I'm about to run into the gym office and

beg a teacher for a safety pin, I actually manage to sink a shot. It's a total brick, and I have no clue how it falls in, but I don't care. Woody slaps me on the back, and all is well. I bend, set, and shoot again, thinking, *I'm on a streak here. One in a row, baby! I'm on fire. Move over, Yao Ming — there's a new Chinese sheriff in town.* Of course, I totally biff on the next three, two of which are air balls. Woody goes to retrieve the second one, and I quickly yank my shorts up to roughly chin level, hoping that my huge overhanging shirt will hide the waistline. But the shirt is so outrageously long that it now goes past the bottoms of my shorts. So I'm shooting baskets in sandals and a freakin' dress. With a nice, casual purse, I'd have quite the look going on.

Woody kicks my feet apart. I bend and shoot. I suck and miss. Woody takes a deep breath. "San, this isn't like you. You have to bear down. Your last shot doesn't matter. Your next shot doesn't matter. Your form is all that matters."

And as my shorts start creeping downward again,

I can't help but think she's definitely in a perfect position to judge my form. I try to blank out my mind like I'm out on my rock. I pretend the sun is on my upturned face, instead of the sickly heatless glare of the fluorescent lights. I pretend I'm all alone in the world, that the girl I like isn't standing inches away from me, filling my nostrils with the scent of oranges and my brain with all kinds of totally non-hoops-related urges, while she's probably getting a good view of my undies. And perhaps most of all, I pretend I am the ball. I am the hoop. I am the hoop and the ball, the rim and the net. We are one thing, the ball and the net and me. One perfect, connected whole.

It's just that the various parts of the perfectly connected whole don't always come into physical contact with each shot.

God, I'm pathetic at this. And my toes are still freezing. The warning bell rings, and Woody says, "Well, we're making progress."

"How are we making progress?"

"Well, we're becoming a better team. We're learning

about each other. Before today, I might have thought you were a Houston Rockets fan! See ya in social studies, partner."

I reach back and yank up my gym shorts.

Do real Zen masters blush? Because fake ones do.

Signs and wonders

That same day in social studies, I walked in just behind Woody and in front of Peter and got myself settled. I was just sitting there, about to take out my journal notebook, minding my own business, when Peter raised his hand and said, "So, Mr. Dowd, remember the other day when you said that there were six Zen patriarchs, and then the dynasty fell apart? Well, I was reading last night about the other branches of Buddhism in these books I got from the library, and the books said that some sects identify their next leader by watching for miracles, or for a child who shows amazing wisdom."

Dowd said, "Yes, that's all true. Did I miss a question in there somewhere, Mr. Jones?"

"Yeah, I mean, yes. The question is, what if there's a seventh patriarch right now walking around the planet waiting to be discovered? There could be, right?"

"Uhh, sure. The Zen tradition doesn't really look for reincarnations of Buddha figures generally, but I suppose anything's possible. Why do you ask?"

"Well, when I was trying to fall asleep last night, I started wondering: What if the seventh Zen patriarch is walking among us right now?"

Then I swear he gave me an evil little grin.

"I'm saying, how would we know? Would he walk across fire or something? Would he be immune to heat and cold? Would he be disguised as someone really poor? Maybe he would have some cool, mystical-sounding name, like 'The Laughing Archer.' I guess I'm asking, what would we look for? Signs and wonders?"

Dowd's eyebrows were knit together, and his twinkle was temporarily subdued. "I'm, uhh, glad that you're taking such an interest in this unit of study, Peter, but I'm somewhat uncomfortable speculating about the theoretical beliefs and practices of a religious group in this way. Please feel free to do some additional research, and see me privately if you have any further questions. And now, if you will all take out your journals . . ."

I bent to remove my notebook from my backpack, and saw with horror what Peter must have been staring at as we had entered the classroom: The journal was pressed up against the clear plastic, with the front cover exposed for the world to see. The front cover where I'd written "The Laughing Archer" across the NAME line in oversized letters.

What in the world was Peter doing? Did this mean he had put the mysterious note in my locker? And if so, why? What was his problem? I suddenly noticed that the girl next to me was looking at the cover of the notebook too. Then she turned away to whisper to the guy behind her. So now what? Were these people going to expect me to walk across hot coals on the school lawn? Or were they just going to laugh at me, San Lee, Freak of the World? I had to say something. I raised my hand.

"Uh, Mr. Dowd? Can I answer Peter?"

"Well . . ."

"Please? It will only take a minute."

"Go ahead. I can see that the lesson-plan gods are against me today."

"Listen, Zen isn't like what Peter said at all. It's not very much concerned with the supernatural — it's about finding wisdom in everyday things. There's this famous Zen story:

"A monk told Joshu, 'I have just entered the monastery. Please teach me.'

"Joshu asked, 'Have you eaten your rice porridge?'

"The monk replied, 'I have eaten.'

"Joshu said, 'Then you had better wash your bowl.'

"At that moment the monk was enlightened."

I paused.

"See? Nobody's looking for a magical new leader — just a new way of seeing."

Dowd said, "Thank you for the very appropriate story, San. Now, I'm hoping we can do some school-type stuff. You know — take some notes? Fill in some blanks?"

I was just wishing someone would help me fill in the blanks in my *life*. But I took out my notebook, just like everybody else.

For the next few days, I tried to just lay low, both at home and at school. I did all my homework, read all of *The Tao of Pooh* in one night, didn't volunteer in class, and avoided spending time alone with my mom or Woody. Or Peter. Or Dowd. Or anyone, actually.

Except in gym. Woody and I were practicing like

crazy. So far our big Zen experiment was not producing visible results, and the end of the marking period wasn't going to wait just because I sucked at foul shooting. I kept telling Woody that Zen archers never worry about accuracy; they just get their form perfectly and the accuracy comes automatically. But she kept saying that Zen archers aren't doing their arching for a major project grade.

Great — the pressure was sure to improve my accuracy, right?

On the Tuesday after my phone call crisis with Mom, Woody and I were getting set up, and all of a sudden, Peter was there. "Betcha can't beat me in a shooting match, Buddha."

I smiled at him. "Bet you're right, Peter. You're a great basketball player."

I got the feeling that wasn't the answer he wanted. He snapped back, "And you're afraid to take my bet."

He had a point. I was just about to admit it, when Woody leaned over and whispered to me, "Do it, San!"

I murmured back, "Why? You know your brother will waste me."

She hissed back, "STEPbrother, San. STEPbrother. And he won't waste you. You've been practicing for days on end. If you beat him in front of everyone, we'll definitely get a good grade."

Was this all I was to her — a grade? I bet she wouldn't force ELL to make a fool of himself in front of a whole gym class just for a project. On the other hand, ELL was probably some superjock in the first place.

Maybe I should step up to the line, I thought. *Of course, it's a total betrayal of the whole Zen concept, letting myself be goaded into shooting for egotistical purposes. But then again, Woody wants me to. Plus, maybe she's right. Maybe I will beat Peter. Yeah, right. And maybe the U.S. invading Iraq was a brilliant idea.*

But Woody was looking and, in the end, that was what mattered. I stepped up. "You call the rules, Peter."

"OK, Buddha. We each shoot ten free throws. Whoever sinks the most, wins. If it's a tie, we shoot one at a time from the top of the key until someone misses. You go first."

You know how sharks swarm in from miles around when they smell blood in the water? This was like that, only the entire gym class was the shark posse, and I was the bloody bucket of chum. While everyone was jostling up to surround us in a boiling sea of carnivorous excitement, Woody leaned in close and whispered to me, "San, you can do this. I know you can."

I turned and looked at her like a rabbit looks into the blades of an approaching lawn tractor. Then I faced the basket and gripped the ball for dear life.

"I'm serious, San. Be the ball. Be the net." She leaned in and kicked my feet apart one final time. Then her lips might have just brushed my ear as she added, "For me, OK?"

Well, there's nothing like a little horribly timed flirting to get a man ready for combat. I took several deep breaths, bent my knees, and shot without even really looking. Everyone cheered. The ball had somehow found its way in. Some huge moose of a kid threw me the rebound. I said to myself, *How does one think about not thinking? Without thinking,* and shot again before I had time to start thinking about thinking about not thinking.

Swish.

Rebound, *swish.*

Rebound, *swish.*

Rebound, *swish.*

Woody whispered to me, "Five-for-five! You're gonna win!"

And as her orangey smell swept into my head, I lost my rhythm. Missed three of my last five. But hey, seven for ten was about six better than my usual. I bounce-passed the ball to Peter. "Thanks for the challenge," I said mildly. "This is fun!" Woody stood next to me, so close that our elbows pushed up against each other every time the crowd moved.

Peter glared at me, stepped up, and sank three in a row. Then someone said, "Hey, Pete — remember that game against Phillipsburg when you were nine-for-nine from the line?"

Guess what? Even star basketball jocks can get

jinxed. Peter missed his next two shots. One more, and we would be tied. Yikes!

Peter looked around, set, and shot. He sank the next three, then missed one. That put him at six-for-nine. If he missed the last shot, I'd win. But if he sank it, we'd be shooting it out with three-pointers. I realized I'd never actually sunk a three-pointer before. Oh, joy.

Peter dribbled and stopped. He started dribbling again, and stopped again. Then he looked at me, said, "It was fun playing with you too," and drained his last shot without even looking. Before I could even fall to the cold gym floor, pound the unfeeling boards with my puny fists, and curse whatever gods there be, Peter stepped back to the top of the key, caught the ball from the Rebound Bison, and shot a perfect three.

The big guy tossed me the ball and Woody smiled at me. It occurred to me that she was getting into this in a big way. I prayed, *Don't let me throw an air ball.* Then I stared at the backboard until my eyes began to blur a bit, bent my knees, and shot. The ball hit the front edge of the rim, bounced up way too high, hit the backboard on the way down, and started rolling around and around the rim. Just watching it spin made me want to hurl. I didn't want to watch, so I turned away.

When everyone started to cheer a second later, I assumed I'd lost. I prepared myself to face Peter, congratulate him in cool Zen fashion, and then try to slink away into the dank and shadowy recesses of the locker room as quickly and quietly as possible. Then Woody slapped me on the back, hard, and said, "Wow, San, I am some kind of Zen teacher!"

Peter had been looking for signs and miracles, and apparently the time had come. We were tied. He looked stunned; I'm sure I did too. But he recovered first. "Nice one, San. Now step aside and watch me put an end to this thing."

Everyone had been chattering frantically among themselves, but when Peter put up his second shot, the silence was complete and instantaneous. Then the rebound guy shouted, "SHORT!" And it was. The ball barely kissed the rim before falling straight down and dribbling slowly away across the gym floor. Someone kicked it back to me, and I was just approaching the line when the warning bell rang. "Oh, well," I announced, "we'll just have to continue this tomorrow."

Peter said, "Not so fast, Buddha. Take this shot."

I was going to lose whether I waited or not, so I figured I'd better make it look like I didn't care. I turned to him and said, "All right, Peter. It's only a friendly contest, right?"

He gave a sickly little nod, and — with amazing showmanship — I flipped the ball as hard as I could over my shoulder backward, in the general direction of the hoop.

Second
helping

On the way to the soup kitchen the next day, Woody was practically bouncing out of her boots. "San, that was so cool! Did you see the look on Peter's face when you beat him *with your back turned?* Oh, that was awesome! You just take everything so calmly. Even when everyone was running up to you and giving high-fives, you were so relaxed about it. And, you know, today all these guys from the basketball B team asked me if you and I could give them free-throw lessons."

"I hope you said no."

"Wellllll . . ."

I stared.

". . . I said maybe."

I stared some more.

"I told them that we were really busy with our charitable work and all, but that we'd let them know if anything changed. But don't you get it? Our project is a total success. You're, like, famous! A seventh grade girl asked me today if I could get her your autograph!"

"What was her name?" I asked, before I could think about it.

"I don't know — Katie something, maybe. Anyway, you don't have any earthly attachments, remember?"

"I was just wondering what her name was. Names are important."

She was looking serious all of a sudden. "By the way, San, before we get to the soup kitchen, I wanted to tell you about the whole name thing: My parents named me Emily — Emily Jane Long — after my mother's mother. But when my mom left, I decided I didn't want to be named after somebody from her side of the family. Plus I didn't feel like the same person anymore, so I just . . . decided to be somebody else."

She bit her lip. "You probably think that's totally stupid, right?"

I could have told her right then. It was an amazing moment: Woody was like me. We were both inventing ourselves from scratch because of our screwed-up parents. I could reveal my secrets to her and she'd understand. I could open my soul to her, and she would embrace me. We could join hands and frolic together through fields of daisies. It would be us against the world. Bonnie and Clyde. Caesar and Cleopatra. Madonna and, uh, everybody.

But I hesitated. I thought about it too long. What would happen with our project if Woody found out I was a fake? The grade was really important to her and so was honesty. Yikes, honesty. She wasn't going to want to frolic in the daisies with the son of a convicted con man. And what about ELL?

She was waiting for me to say something, to tell her she wasn't stupid. "You're not stupid," I said. "You're just stuck in this demented culture that says a person can't change who she is inside. So if you don't like who you were yesterday, you're — I don't know — stuck with yourself. But your way was the Zen way."

She chewed on that one for a while, and then asked, "How is that the Zen way?"

"A great Japanese thinker said, 'Concentrate on and consecrate yourself completely to each day, as though a fire were raging through your hair.'"

"Meaning?"

"All that matters right now is what you do right now."

"Really?" She grinned.

"Honest to Buddha." I grinned back and crossed my eyes. Then she grabbed my hand and started skipping. We almost got hit by an oil truck, but we skipped all the way to the shelter. Then we leaned against the wall with our hands on our knees, gasping for air and laughing. A whole line of people waiting to eat had already formed; we had skipped right past the line. I stopped laughing then. It seemed wrong to be so carefree right in front of all these people who had nothing. Woody looked up and got quiet too. She nudged me with her hip and tilted her head toward the back of the line. Two of the little kids from the week before — a boy and a girl — were pointing at us and cracking up. Suddenly the girl gripped the boy's hand and they started skipping up and down the line. Everyone laughed with them.

The two kids skidded to a stop about a foot from us. The boy said, "Hi, I'm Shaun. I'm the king of skipping," and bowed at the waist. The girl stuck her tongue out at him and told us, "I'm Annie. I'm the *ace* of skipping!" Then she curtsied.

I said, "Nice to meet you. I'm San — whoever that is today."

Woody said, "Hi, it's a pleasure to have your company. I'm Woody, and my hair is on fire!" As we walked away, I heard the boy whisper, "That girl is crazy. They better not be letting her cook the food in there."

Fortunately we were still on dish duty. Which was fun. There was some joking about flaming hair, which led to some moderately intense water fighting, which eventually settled down into real talking. The work went more smoothly, because we knew what we were doing, which let me concentrate on having fun with this amazing girl and watching the sudsy water drip from her shining hair. And on getting hungry. The main course was hamburgers and hot dogs (which also made the cleaning easier, because burgers and dogs have a much lower "glop factor" than spaghetti). The hamburgers smelled great. I couldn't wait to take a huge, juicy, charcoal-y bite of one. As soon as we were done washing, we sat up on the counter and I waited droolingly for our well-earned and beefy reward.

Mildred came in and handed us two heaping plates of burger, pickle, and coleslaw. She cackled, "Wash your bowl, right San?" and was all ready to walk back out when Woody said, "Wait! San can't eat that burger!"

I jerked the delicious bun-enclosed patty away from my wide-open jaws in surprise. "What do you mean, he can't eat the burger?" Mildred asked. "He's a growing boy, and I'm sure all of your horsing around back here has given him quite an appetite. And he probably wants some food too! Heh-heh."

Woody's cheeks turned an appealing reddish-pink. "No, I mean — San doesn't eat meat. He's a Buddhist. And, you know, that makes him a vegetarian."

Crap. She had a point, as far as she knew. Mildred raised one snow-white eyebrow at me, but said, "I'll see what I can scrounge up." After she went back into the kitchen, I made myself say, "Thanks, Woody. I was afraid I'd be having a pickle on a bun for dinner."

She winked at me. Wow, nobody except my one totally senile uncle had ever winked at me before. It looked cuter when she did it, though. "No problem. Got to keep up your strength for foul-shooting. And skipping, of course."

I smiled then, but had trouble maintaining the expression when Mildred reappeared. Carrying a veggie wrap, which she deftly switched for my burger. A veggie wrap? I felt betrayed. What kind of soup kitchen serves veggie wraps anyway?

Have I mentioned how much I hate vegetables? There are only two kinds of eaters in the world, and the Cap'n Crunch fanatics aren't in the same category as the carrot-juice junkies, believe me. But Mildred and Woody were watching. I forced myself to unclench my teeth and let the soggy horror in. Yikes! As my incisors sank into each successive layer, it took all my willpower not to choke the whole thing back onto my plate.

Sadly, it was a fat wrap. There were the mandatory sprouts, which popped in my mouth and shot out foul, dirt-flavored liquid. There was the tortilla itself, which tasted like some horrible mutant off-spring of carrot and spinach. There was something slippery and unspeakably spongy — tofu? A fluffy mushroom? And the whole shebang was drenched in a ghastly ranch dressing that tasted like month-old mayonnaise would taste if you were licking it off of a dead cat's mangy fur. With garlic.

And you know, I chomped down every last morsel before it occurred to me that I could have just eaten my coleslaw.

face-to-face,
toe-to-toe

The next morning I could still taste the sprout-and-garlic horror even after brushing twice, scarfing down a massive dose of Cap'n Crunch, brushing again, and chugging enough mouthwash to sterilize a Port-a-Potty. Do you know how hard it is to meditate when your mouth is a vegetable disaster area?

But then again, I'm San Lee. If cold, rain, poverty, and tragedy couldn't break my concentration, neither could a dead plant sandwich. By this point, sitting zazen had become strangely comfortable for me, and the little indent in my rock where the bottom of my back rested felt like my personal easy chair. When Woody got to school, she found me zoning out. In fact, I was probably about three-quarters of the way to nirvana, and closing fast, when Woody stomped her feet right in front of me.

"Ugh," she groaned, "I hate him!"

"And a good morning to you too, partner. Uh, what are you talking about?"

"My brother, the idiot!"

I couldn't help myself: "STEPbrother, you mean."

She glared at me. "You don't understand, San. Him and his stupid mother. They're ruining my life!"

"OK, Woody, calm down. What happened?"

Note to self: Never tell the girl you like to calm down. "What happened? WHAT HAPPENED? I'll tell you what happened: Peter told my mom that you and I are going out."

Wow, was it hot out here, or was it just me? "Uh, are we?"

"San, I don't think so. Earthly attachments, right? But that's not even the point. The point is that now my wicked stepmom doesn't want me to be with you, unsupervised, every Wednesday. So she said I can't go to the soup kitchen with you anymore."

"But we're not unsupervised there. We're in a building with, like, three hundred people. And our boss is a NUN! What does she think, we're going to be playing tonsil hockey in front of freakin' Mother Teresa?"

Tonsil hockey? Had I really just said tonsil hockey?

Woody snorted, and maybe got a little bit red. "I know, I know. But my parents are total maniacs about keeping me 'safe' from boys until I'm, like, twenty-nine or something."

"Can't you just get Peter to tell her he was wrong? What if we talk to him right now? How immature can he possibly be?"

"We could talk to him now, I guess," Woody said. "Except that a) he went into the building early because he said he had something important to take care of, b) he's incredibly immature, and c) he hates both of us, so he's thrilled that he got me in trouble with his mom."

"Oh." Woody was staring down at her feet, swishing them around in the icy grass. "Uh, why does Peter hate you, exactly?"

"Well, it's a long story. Basically, he thinks my dad broke up his parents' marriage."

"Why?"

"Uh, because my dad broke up his parents' marriage."

"But what does that have to do with you?"

"Nothing. Except for a while his mom tried really hard to be my pal, and Peter refused to spend any time with my dad — so Peter was pretty neglected for about half a year in sixth grade. Which isn't my fault either. It's not like I wanted to hang out and shop with Little Miss Sweetness anyway. All I wanted was my real mom."

"So, where is your real mom?"

"I don't know, San. She's just gone. I mean, she left a mailing address, but she hasn't contacted us once. She took off out of here and as far as I know she hasn't looked back. You're lucky — I bet your family isn't as messed up as mine."

Ha! I didn't know what to say to that one, but the bell saved me. We hurried to be on time, and by the time we got to her homeroom, the moment was past. On the way to my locker, I thought about the irony: I could have totally bonded with Woody about the missing-parent thing, but then she would have hated me for all the other stuff I had lied about. Plus our situations were a little different: She wanted her mom back, and I wished my dad would stay locked up forever.

I had a sad feeling that neither of us would get what we wanted.

In my locker, I found another Zen note:

HOW SHALL I GRASP IT? DO NOT GRASP IT. THAT WHICH REMAINS WHEN THERE IS NO MORE GRASPING IS THE SELF.

— PANCHADASI

What did that mean? Who had put it there? And why? It hit me that Peter had gone into the school before everyone else. *He* must have been my secret note-stalker. Which meant he must have seen me that night in the library. So why was he putting these stupid messages in my locker? Was he trying to make me crack and admit I was a total phony? Then why didn't he just confront me? I needed to know.

I sat steaming-mad all through English class, which was interesting because we spent the whole period talking about a big idea in *The Tao of Pooh*: wu wei, or "without doing, causing, or making." Wu wei is a lot like "thinking without thinking." The idea is that you have to let things roll off your back and go with the flow. This was strange: "Wu" means "without," and the Chinese symbol for wei comes partly from a grasping claw. So you should relax and stop grasping — like the quote in my locker. According to Taoism, things will always work out if you do that. Yeah, right. When someone is trying to sabotage your whole life, how can you let that roll off your back?

Well, I'd show him. Nobody stops me from washing dishes if I want to wash dishes. My mom couldn't stop me, sprouts couldn't stop me, and I'd be darned if some demented stepbrother was going to stop me. I had to come up with a plan to get me and Woody back into the soup business. But first I had to confront Peter, even if he was scary huge.

I caught up to him in the hallway on the way to lunch. "Hello, Peter," I spat. "Visited any interesting lockers lately?"

"What are you talking about?"

"Oh, I think you know."

"Uh, I don't."

"Oh, sure you don't. Listen, Peter, I know you know."

"What?"

"About my secret. Just tell me what I have to do to keep you from blabbing it everywhere."

"What? You're ashamed of your secret, San?"

"I didn't say that."

"Then why can't I mention it to my own mom?"

Dang. His *mom* knew too?

"And why does Woody deny the whole thing completely? What are you two ashamed of? How great is your little relationship if you have to pretend it doesn't exist?"

Oh. Ooooohhhhhh. Peter didn't know about my Zen act. He just really thought Woody and I were going out. "We're friends, Peter. OK? Haven't you ever heard of that? It's when two people just enjoy each other's company. And why is it your business? Why do you hate your sister so much, anyway?"

Now Peter looked mad. "Hate her? *Hate* her? I love her, San. We've been living in the same house for four years, and we were friends before that too. How could I hate my own sister? Geez."

"Then why would you go around making trouble for her on purpose?"

"I'm not making trouble for her — I'm saving her from trouble."

"How do you figure that?"

"Because you're trouble, San. Stay away from my sister. You have no idea what she's been through, OK? She doesn't need some Zen weirdo to come breezing into town and mess her up all over again. And it doesn't take a big mystical insight to realize that that's what's going to happen."

"Peter, it's not like that. I —"

"It's not like that? Then why can't you just admit you like each other? And what's the big secret about your locker?"

Oopsie, guess that might come back to haunt me.

"Look, I'm just saying, I know you're going to hurt Emily. And then I'm going to hurt you."

"You're wrong, Peter!"

"No, I really am going to hurt you."

"Not about that — I'm sure you could crush me.

But I'm not going to hurt your stepsister. I care about her."

"Oh, yeah? Then ask her why she started calling herself 'Woody.'"

"I know why she started to call herself that. She didn't want to be named after anyone from her mom's family, so she changed her name to Woody."

"Yeah, but why Woody? Why not Jane? Why not Jennifer? Why not, I don't know, E-Lo? You don't know as much as you think you do, Buddha. You just don't."

And that was it. He walked away, leaving me with a threat and a riddle. My heart was pounding and my palms were soaked, but I couldn't waste any time sitting around and worrying. I had to put my "Save the Wednesdays" plan into motion. I put on my game face, and headed over toward the jock tables.

twigs

After school I had way too much to think about. I was feeling way hyper, so I took a long, slow path home around the library and through what passed for a downtown in Harrisonville. I found myself on a street I'd never seen before, with a bunch of townhouses leading to a dead end. Just past the end of the street, there was a little hidden park with a stream running through it. I figured I'd cut through and try to find my way back home, but then I decided to sit on a rock by the water for a while. There was still a pretty big chunk of time before my mom would be home, and I didn't feel like being cooped up in the apartment alone.

No, it was much better to be sitting in a random park alone.

The rock wasn't quite as comfy as "my" rock, but I had to admit the setting was nice. I must have spent twenty minutes watching two twigs tumbling around in the current between a stone and a little peninsula of mud and getting lost in my worries. First, there was the ELL thing. Woody's first and last initials were E and L, so it crossed my mind for a second that *she* might be ELL — but she'd said her middle name was Jane. I toyed with the idea that maybe I'd seen the letters wrong on the back of her assignment sheet. Could I have mistaken a *J* for an *L*? But there was just no way, especially since it was next to another L, and the whole thing was written several times.

I sighed. Maybe she hadn't finished writing when I'd come across the paper. Maybe she was filling in each heart one letter at a time, the way little kids copy their spelling five-times-each homework words. So I started thinking of some names that started with "ELL": Ellington. Ellery. Ellbert.

Ellvis?

Nah. Woody had to be a better speller than that. Plus, I knew from my mom that nobody liked the Beatles AND Elvis; it was always one or the other.

OK, maybe "ELL" was the end of the person's name, and she was going backward: Tyrell. Martell. Shell. Smell. Bell.

Roswell.

This was ridiculous. I had no clue. I started thinking about the other issues of my busy day, like what I had gotten myself into at the athletes' table, and what Peter had been trying to tell me about Woody's name, and what it would feel like when he finally got around to smashing my face in. My thoughts were tumbling as aimlessly as the two little twigs.

And then I heard a shuffling sound. I looked up, and there was a shrimpy little kid standing next to the rock, carrying a backpack that might have weighed more than he did. "Excuse me?" he said in a little not-yet-changing voice.

"Uh, yes?"

"Umm, that's my rock. I mean, I don't own it or anything, but it's where I come to sit sometimes when . . ."

"When what?"

He looked at me with total despair. "When I can't go home." Oh, boy. The little guy was bumming bigtime about something.

I moved over. It was a big rock. "Here," I said, "Have a seat."

He did.

We stared at the twigs for a while, and then he spoke. "Hi, my name is Justin. I'm in sixth grade. You're that Buddha guy, San Lee, right?"

I just looked at him.

"I can tell by your, um, shoes. I mean, you're the guy with the three-pointer, aren't you? Oh, man, everybody on the bus was talking about it. They said you totally *schooled* Peter Jones. That must have been so awesome." He paused. "But, uh, weren't you scared to beat him?"

I looked at the kid some more.

"I mean, I sometimes go to the YMCA after school. And I remember last year when Jones was in seventh grade, the basketball team got killed in a home game, and Peter missed like seven of his last eight shots. This eighth grader laughed at him at the Y the next day, and . . ."

Justin shuddered. "Oh, man. I don't like to talk about it. I don't even want to *think* about it."

There was a long pause before he continued. "I have to say, though — those janitors at the Y did a really good job of mopping up afterward."

Excellent. This kid was a total bundle of joy. I was starting to get light-headed. It was definitely time for a subject change. "Hey, Justin, you said you can't go home. How come?"

He stared at the water for so long that I thought the twigs might get waterlogged and sink before he answered. "Well, you have to promise not to tell anyone, OK?"

Uh-oh. Did this little kid have abusive parents? Or maybe they had a drug problem. I couldn't promise not to tell if Justin might be in danger. On the other hand, maybe this was the one time when he was willing to talk about it.

Good God.

I didn't say anything, but Justin plowed ahead with his confession: "I have this big sister. She's in high school. And she has this boyfriend. And he likes to come over after school sometimes. And then they kick me out for an hour. I set the little timer on my watch — see?" He held it out to me. "And if I ever come home early, my sister said she would yank out my liver with a fork and serve it to me for dinner."

Nice. This was, like, the blood-and-guts family.

"So here you are," I said.

"So here I am."

We watched the twigs some more while I tried not to giggle about Justin's problem. Then he said, "There's another thing bothering me too. It's even worse than the first thing."

I worked on keeping a straight face. "Tell me," I intoned.

"Well, there's this girl in my homeroom. Her name is Amber. I think she might like me, but I'm not sure. I mean, sometimes she acts like she hates me. And sometimes she acts like she likes someone else. But then sometimes she's, like, all flirting with me. The other day I think she was purposely touching my shoulder in the lunch line, and she was kind of singing under her breath, 'I have a se-cret. I have a se-cret.' But the next period, she threw a tic tac at my head in math."

Justin looked at me. I looked at the twigs.

"Well?" he said.

"Well, what?"

"Well, does she like me or not?"

"How should I know?"

"*Duh.* You're the Zen guy. Everyone says you have wisdom and stuff. This should be an easy one for you to solve, right?"

"You'd be surprised. Girls are tricky."

"Even for you?"

"Even for me."

"Wow." He looked awestruck. "So, what should I do?"

"Have you tried asking her?"

"Asking her?"

"Yeah, you know, like, 'What's your secret?'"

He looked even more awestruck. "So, you're saying I would just *ask* her the secret?"

I nodded solemnly.

"And she might, like, tell me?"

I nodded again. "Sometimes, things need a little push in the right direction. Look, do you see those two twigs?"

"Yeah?"

"Well, they're spinning around and around, kind of trapped in each other's orbit, right?"

"Uh, OK."

"Watch." I grabbed a stone from the ground next to me. I took careful aim, and then tossed it into the water, right between the twigs and the little peninsula. The waves from the rock nudged the twigs away . . . away a little more . . . and then the twigs spun out from behind their rock and into the open water.

"Whoa. That's . . . that's . . . whoa. You really are the Zen master, aren't you?"

I smiled. The twigs glided away downstream.

one hand washes
the other

When my mom finally got home from work that night, she had a big surprise for me. "Guess what, San?" she said, breathless from climbing the stairs with packages. "I got my first big overtime bonus check today, so I went shopping at lunch. I finally got you a winter coat. I just wish we could have afforded this sooner." She whipped out a bright green-and-yellow parka that looked like the uniform for a special all-blind unit of the ski patrol. "Since we're already partway through the season, it was on clearance. I can't believe nobody grabbed it up — we're so lucky! And that's not all — I got you gloves too."

Great — these were a brilliant white. Who wears white winter gloves? What was it, winter mime season? But I knew she was really excited to be able to get this stuff for me, so I tried to look cheerful about it. At least until she busted out with one final item.

"And . . . ta-da! Sneakers! Good ones! Remember when you made me promise I wouldn't buy you sneakers until we could afford name-brand ones? I still think you were being ridiculous, but — I got you real Nike high-tops. Your favorite color, red. I remember you saying that you have basketball in gym right now, so these should be perfect!" Mom stopped when she glanced at my face. "Uh, honey, what's the matter? You look like you just swallowed a lemon."

They were nice basketball shoes. *Very* nice basketball shoes. And, other than the revolting color scheme, my mom had totally come through for me. But how was I supposed to be all Zen with this deluxe set of spanking-new, name-brand outerwear? "Oh, it's nothing, Mom. My stomach hurts, that's all. I must have gotten a bad carton of milk at lunch or something. But this is great. Really. Thanks. I think I'll just go lie down now, if that's okay with you."

She looked kind of crestfallen, like I'd ruined her whole shopping victory parade. But I couldn't help it. How on earth was I going to explain this at school? I took the packages and retreated to my room to think. While I was thinking, I tried everything on. The sneakers felt so incredibly soft and warm that it was like my feet had died and gone to heaven. But I didn't care about that; all I cared about was how I was going to change out of them every day on the way to school, hide them all day, and then change again on my way home. OK, I was a smart and crafty individual. I would come up with something, right?

The first thing that came to mind was just stuffing my sandals in my backpack before bed, wearing the sneakers out of the apartment, changing back into the sandals outside, and then doing the reverse in the afternoon. Except that my stupid backpack was see-through. Darn that stupid school security! Then I thought maybe I could somehow stuff the sandals in between notebooks or something in the middle of the backpack so my mom wouldn't see them. So I tried that, and it worked great . . . until I realized that the gigantic new sneakers would have to fit in there once I changed out of the sandals. Plus, what was I going to do with the coat? It was huge and puffy, and the color was bright enough to be seen from outer space.

Nothing is ever simple.

But after about twenty minutes of pacing the six feet of available floor space in my room, I did come up with something that might work. I needed to take a walk in order to try it. I threw on the toasty new coat and headed out with my sandals hidden in my armpit. Mom stopped me, naturally.

"Where are you going, San? I thought you didn't feel well. I'm making you some broth with rice."

"That's great, Mom. I'll eat it when I get back. I'm just going for a little stroll. I thought the exercise might help. You know, work the poisons out of my system. And, uh, try out my awesome new clothes."

I think she knew something was fishy, because her forehead was all wrinkled up, but what was she going to do — keep me inside to punish me for saying I didn't feel so hot?

Yup, she was. "Sanny, are you going to meet with your little girlfriend or something? Because you're grounded, remember?"

"Mom, Jesus, I'm taking a walk. A plain old ordinary walk, by myself. Even grounded kids get to take a walk. Even prisoners get exercise time."

Oh, crap. I did *not* just mention prisoners.

She sighed. "That's true. But if you're not back in ten minutes, Warden Mom is going to come find you."

Wow, she had just made a prison joke. In some ways, we were getting pretty used to our little situation. "Thanks, Mom. I promise I'll be back in twenty minutes."

"Fifteen," she snapped back at me.

"Deal," I said, and got out of there.

As soon as I was on the stairs, I started scouting the terrain. What I needed was a hidden place where I could stash the winter gear every morning, and pick it back up every afternoon. This was ridiculous: I found myself feeling along the wood paneling of the staircase wall, like there might be a secret hidden parka compartment. But all I found was a splinter.

Then I had the brilliant idea that maybe there was a safe little alcove or something outside. I walked around the whole perimeter of the apartment house, but at least in the early winter darkness, I didn't see anything obvious. Not that I'd expected a steel-reinforced camouflaged shed with EMERGENCY

FOOTWEAR SHELTER on the side or anything, but a hollowed-out space in the side wall of the building would have worked fine. Oh, well. I crossed the street to see whether there was anything in the playground — like maybe I could bury the stuff in the sandbox every morning. But as I was kneeling and poking the sand with a stick to see how deep it was, the same old lady who'd yelled at me when I was stealing sand the last time I'd been there came around a bend in the hedges and said, "You again? What are you doing this time?"

"Checking the depth of the sandbox with this stick I found."

"And why are you doing that, young man?"

Well, I thought, *I'm looking for a place to hide my secret stash of high-grade cocaine, because my mom only lets me keep bombs, guns, and heroin in my room.* I said, "Well, I'm looking for a place to hide my coat, gloves, and sneakers because everyone at my school thinks I'm a Zen master. Is that OK?"

She said, "Sure. Just try not to hide them behind my invisible flying saucer, all right? Never know when

167

the mothership might call me home." It figured —
everyone's a wiseguy. As she shuffled away humming
merrily, I shook my head and resumed my sandbox
inspection. But there was just no way I could get the
whole ensemble hidden in there without somebody
finding it. Plus there was a distinct cat-pee scent
emanating from the sand this evening, and there was
no way that would be healthy. As I turned to go back
home in defeat, I spied a half-buried drainpipe leading from the edge of the mulch area into a flood
ditch thing. I couldn't really see into it too well, but
it appeared to go in at least a few feet. As an added
bonus, the opening of the pipe faced into the ditch,
so no one on the playground would be able to see
my stuff.

It wasn't great, but neither was wearing the Bozo
the Ski Clown outfit to school.

With my mission accomplished, I hurried to get
back upstairs before my mother called out the
National Guard. She looked relieved that I didn't
have any obvious lipstick marks or hickeys, and gave
me a nice bowl of rice soup to warm me up. Of

course, she didn't know that The Laughing Archer doesn't feel heat and cold, but the gesture was nice.

I said good-bye to my mom while she was brushing her teeth the next morning, and shoved my sandals in a black garbage bag before I left the house. I raced across the street, got my sandals out of the bag, switched them for my sneakers by standing on one foot at a time like a flamingo, and then stuffed my coat and gloves in there. The whole bag fit into the mouth of the pipe perfectly, and I pushed it in as far as my arm could reach.

I felt a lot lighter as I turned and headed off to school. I figured, what could possibly go wrong?

For a couple of days, nothing went wrong at all. The hiding place worked great, and I had lunch with Woody every day. Our project was coming together really well, and we spent about ten minutes of each social studies period huddled in a corner writing up our basketball results and the story of our soup kitchen experiences. I could have sworn Woody was sitting closer to me than she really needed to, and I kept thinking about the advice I had given Justin, but then I would tell myself that ELL was out there some-where, and that I should try to concentrate on the work. My Wednesday plan was almost ready to be unleashed. I was memorizing quotes from my Zen books every night, and I was pretty sure my helpers were lined up. So Woody and I would still have our dishwashing time together.

Things weren't perfect, of course. Peter occasion-ally bumped into me and said, "Ask her yet?" And I couldn't do anything but look down and away. Also, every once in a while my mom would remind me that sooner or later she wanted me to talk to my dad, or that she couldn't wait much longer to meet my "special friend." Oh, and I was still waiting for my past to pop up and ruin my whole deluded new life.

But hey, you can't have everything, right?

On Tuesday at the rock, Woody greeted me with, "Hey, San, what's the plan for tomorrow? I've been working on my stepmom for days, and she's not budging. I even went to my dad, but he said, 'Oh, you can't go feed the parasites anymore? Good! One day you'll see that giving handouts never saved anybody.' Which I think means he's not going to be overruling the Witch anytime soon."

"You know, Woody, there's this cool new trend of saying good morning before you launch into the heavy stuff. Everybody's doing it. Maybe you could, uh, join in?"

"San Lee, neither one of us is a big joiner, in case you hadn't noticed. So I repeat, what's the plan? I really don't want to let Sister Mary Clare down. And, um, I have fun there with you."

I didn't know what to say.

"Don't you have fun with me?"

"Uh, yeah, of course I do. I was just, um, thinking. You know."

"No, I don't know. So why don't you share your thoughts with the class?"

She's so cute when she's sarcastic. Is that weird? Whatever. I told her the plan. And when gym period rolled around, it was launch time.

I dressed as fast as I could and waited under my netless basket in the dark corner. Woody got to me first, and then four of the guys from the basketball

B team gathered around, looking nervous. It was showtime.

"Gentlemen," I said in my quiet-yet-firm Zen master voice, "do you all have your parents' permission for tomorrow afternoon?"

They nodded, except for the huge kid who'd been the rebounder at my contest with Peter. He asked, "Can you remind me what working in a soup kitchen has to do with becoming a better foul shooter?"

I looked around at the little assemblage of second-rate jocks. They looked at me. "Karma. Now, are you in or out?"

He clearly had no clue what I was talking about, but on the other hand, what did he have to lose? After a few seconds, he gave the tiniest little nod I've ever seen, but it was enough. Bison Boy was in. Woody smiled big and lined the guys up. She gave them a whole pep talk about proper form, and being the ball, and yada yada. They looked sort of doubtful — well, totally doubtful — but the Bison got set to shoot. Woody kicked his feet apart a bit, and he bent his knees. Then, just as he was about to release the ball, I shouted, three inches from his ear, "HAI!"

He missed by a mile and a half, and turned to glare at me. But everyone else was cracking up, and the tension was broken. "Why'd you do that?" he spat at me.

"The obstacle is the path."

"What does that mean?"

"It's like saying the path is the obstacle."

"What are you *talking* about?"

"You know, the reverse side also has a reverse side."

He still looked mad, and now his brain was all jammed up too. He was suffering from a clear case of mental constipation. Woody threw him the ball. "Just shoot again, OK, Mike? Trust me. Just shoot again."

Mike the Moose set. I wiped the sweat from my palms while everyone was watching him. Woody kicked. Mike crouched. But just as he was about to release the ball, he flinched away from me. And missed by a mile. The rest of the team giggled, uneasily. Was this too much? Were we losing them?

Mike said, "Why'd you ruin my shot again?"

I said, "What do you mean? I did nothing."

"Yeah, but I was waiting for you to yell."

"What does my yelling have to do with your shooting?"

"You distracted me by, uh, not yelling."

"OK," I said. "I didn't realize my not yelling was so loud. I won't not yell at you this time. I promise."

He set. Woody kicked. His legs sprang into action. I shouted, "HAI!"

The ball hit the rim and bounced off to the left. "Better," I said. "Try again."

We went through this whole thing maybe three more times before Mike's first shot went in. Then he missed two more before sinking three straight. Within fifteen minutes or so, Mike was shooting maybe eighty percent no matter what I did.

Woody took the ball from him and said, "Next!"

As some short, stubby kid stepped into place, Mike came over to me. "I don't understand what you did, but it actually worked. How did you do that?"

I gave him the half smile. "I did nothing."

"Oh, come on! I just want to understand."

"If you understand, things are just as they are; if you do not understand, things are just as they are."

He groaned. "So you're saying there are no answers?"

"Mike," I said gently, "there were no questions."

The short kid bent his knees. Mike jumped in his face and yelled, "HAI!"

Service for Seven,
and a hundred feet in the air

You know what? Some jocks make great waiters. Mildred and Sister Mary Clare were overjoyed to have the basketball guys helping out and put them to work right away serving food in the dining hall. For weeks, everything was perfect: The team's shooting was improving dramatically — although that would turn out to be almost a bad thing later — and they were all very happy with Woody and me. After that first day of training, enough other members of the team got involved so that, even with the usual life stuff going on, we always managed to get five helpers to the soup kitchen. I asked Mildred one week why the hoops guys were always out front, while Woody and I were always in a back room alone, and she winked at me. "Why, Mr. Lee," she said, "I'd think a smart boy like you might figure out that being left alone with a pretty girl week after week is its own reward. Now stop asking so many questions before I send in a couple of sweaty athletes to help out in here!"

Now that there were so many other kids helping out, Woody's stepmom was allowing her to continue at the soup kitchen, and was even still driving me home every week. One day in the car, Mrs. Long asked me if my mother would perhaps like to come to their house for a monthly PTA tea meeting, "If she speaks English well enough to feel comfortable." I said that yes, my mom's English skills were sufficiently well-developed for PTA tea purposes, but that unfortunately, she worked full-time. When Mrs. Long replied, "Yes, I'd imagine it's terribly hard for immigrants to get ahead in this country nowadays," I had to bite on the inside of my cheek to keep from laughing. But I kept quiet, and the rides kept coming.

School was going great, my mom was leaving me alone, I was semi-famous as the "Zen Guy," I was getting to spend tons of time with Woody — for a while there, it all seemed too easy. Well, duh. Of course it was too easy. Life is suffering, remember?

Everything started to unravel the day I finally got up the nerve to ask Woody how she got the name. We were supposed to be putting the final touches on our project for social studies, but ours had been done for days. So we were pretending to color our poster masterpiece, titled "Zen and the Art of Free Throws," but were really talking about personal stuff.

"San," Woody said. "Did you ever notice that you never tell me anything about your life?"

"No, I, uh, never noticed that. What do you want to know?"

"Like what does 'San' mean? Is it some kind of mystical thing?"

"Nope. It means 'three.'"

She looked at me and waited for more. When I didn't continue, she asked, "That's it? Just 'three'? Not 'three pandas running'? Not 'three blind mice'? Not 'shoots for three, and scores! The crowd goes wild! And there goes the buzzer — we're into overtime!'"

"Nope. Just three." I couldn't tell her what my mom had once told me: that San was a name typically given to third children in China, so I was probably given up for adoption because my real family couldn't keep a third kid. That wouldn't be a good line of conversation at all. "How about you? Why Woody? I mean, you already told me why not Emily — but not why you chose the name Woody over every other name in the world."

She must have known I was changing the subject away from myself again, but she let me, for the moment. "Well, my mom's family dropped us completely when she left, so I didn't want to be associated with my grandma, right? But I still wanted a connection to my mom. And just before Mom left — when we didn't even know she was going to leave — she bought me a present. I walked home from the school bus stop one day and found her wrapping up something at the kitchen table. My snack was sitting out waiting for me; I still remember, it was vanilla pudding with Oreos crumbled on top and half a glass of milk. Anyway, she was sitting there cutting the ribbon for the gift, and when she looked at me, it looked like she'd been crying. I asked what was going on, and she told me I'd get the present in a couple of days — not that she'd give it to me in a couple of days, but that I'd get it in a couple of days. That was a Monday, and when I got home on Thursday the box was on the table with a note that said she couldn't do this anymore — whatever 'this' was — and that the present was her favorite music in the world. So what was I going to do? I opened the wrapping and found a set of Woody Guthrie CDs inside. She used to play folk music around the house all the time, so I knew a lot of the songs. When Dad got home three hours later, he found me sitting there at the table, crying and listening to Woody Guthrie.

"So when I started guitar lessons the next year, I asked my teacher to show me how to play a bunch of the songs. And here we are. I used to think that my mom would be so impressed with me when she came back if I could play all of her favorite songs. But I've been playing these songs for a couple of years now, and she hasn't come back yet."

"Wow. I'm sorry, Woody."

"Yeah, me too. I actually . . . can I tell you something really dorky?"

"Nothing you could tell me would seem dorky to me."

"Well, I recorded myself playing a bunch of Woody Guthrie songs three weeks ago, and mailed the DVD to my mom. You inspired me to do it, San."

"*I* did? How in the world did I inspire you to do something so fearless?"

"Oh, come on. It was the day after you beat Peter in the foul-shooting contest. We were on the way to the shelter and you said that thing about the fire burning in your hair. Remember? 'All that matters right now is what you do right now'? So even though my mom hadn't come back or gotten in touch, I decided I could send her a message right then. You kind of, I don't know, showed me I could forgive her, in a way."

Wow, Woody really believed in me. Nobody had ever believed in me before, nobody had ever given me that kind of power. Thank God I hadn't told her to jump off a cliff or eat yellow snow, or something. And the funny thing was, I believed in her too, but my belief was right and hers was wrong. She was forgiving, and I was hiding.

"That's not dorky, it's amazing. *You're* amazing."

"Yeah, well, Peter didn't think it was so amazing. He said I'm crazy and that I should just shut up and be happy with the parents I *have*. Maybe he's right. Maybe I was insane to do it. But I sent the package anyway."

A shadow fell over us. Dowd rumbled, "Hello, Miss Long, Mr. Lee. I'm overjoyed to see that you are enjoying a bonding moment, but perhaps you could get back to pretending your project is still in progress?"

His eyes were in full twinkle. "By the way, Mrs. Romberger at the public library has been raving about your research skills, San — and your volunteer efforts at the soup kitchen, as well. Keep up the good work."

He strode away to stop two kids who were playing catch with their model Chinese pagoda project, and Woody looked at me. "Research skills? What are you researching?"

"Long story."

She leaned on the desk between us and put her chin on both hands. "I'd love to hear it."

Yikes! I had to say something. But what? How was I going to weasel my way out of this one?

Apparently, with a little help from Mother Nature. All of a sudden, Woody pulled back in horror, made a little squeaking noise, and pointed to my right. There was a centipede on the arm of the girl next to me, who saw Woody's gesture and looked down. The girl screamed. Her partner screamed. The girl whipped her arm up over her head, causing the centipede to tumble high in the air and down toward her partner's hair. The partner fell backward in her chair, and her feet whacked the edge of their desk. Their huge papier-mâché Buddha flew about a foot off their desk and landed on the floor with a sickening crunch.

They both looked right at me for a split second, and the partner said, "Oops. Sorry, San."

I said, "No problem. The great master, Lin Chi, said, 'If you meet the Buddha, kill the Buddha.' Although, come to think of it, I'm guessing that was just a metaphor."

They both looked puzzled and relieved at the same time, at least until Woody said, "Oh, my God! There it is!"

And there it was, all right. The centipede was now

on the partner's purse. The screaming started up again, and Woody said, "San! Take care of it!"

I couldn't help it. I shouted, "ME? I can't kill that thing!"

She looked at me like I was Prince Charming. "Oh, I know, San. Your Buddhist reverence for all living things, right?"

No, I thought, *my wussy disgust for poisonous things with way too many legs.* "Uh, right."

"You're not the only one who knows how to do research, San Lee. Now take that bug outside before someone steps on it."

Sure enough, about five different guys, including Peter, were closing in on the revolting creature at an alarming rate. If I didn't act fast, this girl's handbag was going to have a thin coating of crunchy special sauce — and Woody was going to think I didn't revere the centipede.

Isn't it funny how life sucks a lot?

"OK," I said commandingly. "I'll get him. Stand back, everybody. We, uh, don't want to scare the little guy any worse than he already is." Or, you know, than *I* already was. I crouched down so the bug bag was at eye level and gingerly lifted the bag's strap off the back of the girl's chair. I looked at the centipede. The centipede waved its loathsome pincers at me. I looked at Dowd, who was standing behind Woody.

"Um, Mr. Dowd? May I please take this insect outside and set it free?" I held up the bag, and Dowd said, "Sure, San. I think that's very noble of . . ." He didn't finish, because he was distracted by the sight of the centipede doing a kamikaze backflip off the bag's zipper, caroming off the girl's cell phone, and landing on the hardwood floor at a dead hundred-foot run. This caused a whole lot of frenzied activity. All the girls were jumping up on chairs like I wanted desperately to do, but all the boys started cheering, "Go, San!" and "Get him, Buddha!" Some kid even called out, "Kill the bug, San!" Which was pretty entertaining, because maybe ten people instantly gave him dirty looks, like, "Don't you know about San's Buddhist reverence for all life? Moron!"

Ah, fame. Well, my fans wanted a show, so I had to give them one. With the speed and dexterity of a bird of prey — well, a vegetarian bird of prey — I snatched up an oversized piece of construction paper from a desk and started chasing that little sucker around the classroom until he fled under Dowd's desk. Just as he was about to disappear into the safety of Dowd's briefcase, I swept the edge of the paper under him from behind, tripping at least sixty of his little legs. I had the centipede! I folded up the edges of the paper so that it was like an upside-down pup tent, and Mister Bug was at my mercy.

Of course, every nerve in my body was screeching, *THROW THE BUG! RUN! RU-U-UN!* But Dowd was watching. Woody was watching. Peter was watching. Very carefully I sealed the tent by crumpling up the edges in one fist. I waved a jaunty good-bye to the class with the other hand and headed out of the room into the hall. Once out of sight, I allowed myself to sag against the lockers for a second and gasp desperately for air. Newsflash: I was HOLDING A CENTIPEDE! One minute I'd been having a deep heart-to-heart with Woody, and the next I was stuck in a wildlife documentary. I just hoped it wasn't going to end like that horrible one where the bear researcher gets mauled by grizzlies.

I took one last deep breath, and then ran like a madman for the stairs. You could probably have heard the *smack-smack* of my sandals against my soles from about a mile away as I booked it out of the building, but it wasn't loud enough to drown out the little popping noises the centipede's body was making as it bounced around inside my paper trap. I stopped on the grass just outside the back door of the school and looked at the paper, realizing that I was totally alone out there. I could put the whole thing down and then jump up and down on it until it looked like the world's goriest art project. Or I could just leave it there, run back in, and say I'd taken care of everything.

In fact, I admit it: I did drop my little package and take a few steps backward away from it. But then it occurred to me that I was supposed to have this reverence for all living things. I mean, Woody really believed I had it. I couldn't just walk away and leave the poor little bug to die in his paper prison.

I stepped back up to the paper. I tried to sort of prod it open with my foot. But of course that didn't work in the least. The only way I was going to free my venomous little amigo was with my hands. "Stupid freakin' reverence for all living things," I muttered. Bending way down, my fingers trembling, I reached for the paper.

got
zen?

Spring came early in my eighth grade year — or at least that's what everyone told me. In Texas we hadn't particularly had seasons, so this was a bit new to my experience. But the trees got leaves again, the flowers bloomed, birds were suddenly all over the place — and I found myself thinking about Woody even more than usual. Teachers everywhere talk about spring fever, but I'd always thought I was immune, that I was just sort of mildly annoying to my teachers all year-round in an even kind of way. That year proved me wrong. It sounds like some cheeseball movie montage, but every bird song reminded me of Woody's voice; every flower was the blossomy scent of her hair; every chirping insect made me feel —

Well, OK. I have to say that every chirping insect still pretty much made me want to climb up in my mom's lap and cry. But the rest of the spring stuff was true. Woody had really changed me. I had faced a horrible childhood fear because of her belief in me. She had taken a massive risk by mailing her mother that DVD because of her belief in me. I guess one thing I was understanding for the first time is that faith is contagious. And Woody and I had such a bad case of it that we'd been infecting people everywhere we went. Except for Peter, who seemed to be immune.

The rest of the school, though, had a serious, critical case of faith-itis. The sickest people of all were the members of the basketball B team. In fact, they were in the late stages of Zen fever, so much so that they'd done something insane. They had challenged the A team to a game — a game they planned to win. It was like I had started a snowball rolling down a hill, and now the snowball was growing and growing as it tumbled out of my grasp — toward a humongous cliff.

Nobody told me that any of this was going on, of course. If the guys had come to me and said they planned to beat the A team in a basketball game, I would have told them there was no way, that they were the B team for a reason. All right, maybe I couldn't tell them that all of my Zen teachings were a total load of BS, but I could have tried to talk them out of this team suicide mission somehow.

But the first I knew of the whole thing was when I walked into school one day with Woody and saw a poster of a yin–yang on the stairwell doors. It was black and white, on a brilliant red background, with no writing whatsoever. I said to Woody, "Hey, check that out. What do you think it's for?"

She looked away. "I don't know, a club maybe?"

"Wait a minute! You know what this is about, don't you?"

"I might." She was trying really hard not to smile, but not quite hard enough.

"Come on, tell me! What's it for?"

"You'll see, San. For now, how about using your famous Zen detachment and patience?"

"But . . . but . . ."

"You'll see, San. I promise!" And with that, she slipped into homeroom.

There were three more of the posters on the hall-way walls between Woody's door and mine. I thought hard. Maybe my English teacher had put them up to coincide with the end of *The Tao of Pooh*. Maybe somebody in one of Dowd's classes was doing this as a project. But on the other hand, maybe Peter was putting them up to increase the amount of pressure and attention I was getting. And maybe a strange race of alien beings had sent them as a message of brotherhood to all earthlings.

All I could do was wonder.

In English class, we had our end-of-book essay test for *The Tao of Pooh*. It was bizarre how all the parts of my life were overlapping all of a sudden; one of the questions was: *As you have learned, the essence of Taoism is the idea that one should walk the middle path between extremes, as symbolized by the yin–yang sign. How might this apply to your own experiences?* I had to roll that one around in my mind a bit, so I answered everything else first. Then I came back to it and started writing about my dad. And Woody.

The next day when we got to school, the yin–yang posters all said GOT ZEN? Woody raised an eyebrow at me. I said, "Are you ready to tell me what this is about?"

"Nope."

"Are you ready to give me a hint?"

"Nope."

"You know, the yin–yang isn't even originally a Zen sign. It's Taoist."

"Wow."

"Are you going to tell me anything? Anything at all? Are you even listening to me right now?"

"Nope. Nope. Yup."

She blew her hair out of her eyes, grinned, and popped into her homeroom.

In gym that day, my disciple, Bison Mike, finally laid the truth on me: The posters were advertisements in the making. He told me that the team, along with Woody, had come up with this plan as a fund-raiser. Then he looked at me like I was supposed to pat him on the head and give him a cookie.

I argued that the whole thing was nuts, that they weren't ready to play the game. He argued back that this wasn't about winning or losing; it was about making money for the cause. I asked, "How much money does a middle school basketball team need anyway?"

He looked hurt, then maybe a little mad. "WE don't need the money, San. You know that. But we thought — I mean, Woody said — I mean, we and Woody —"

"You and Woody what?"

"It was supposed to be a surprise for you. We thought how great it would be if we could raise a lot of money for the soup kitchen. Don't you think so? Woody said you'd be pumped for this."

Oh, great. Now if I kept fighting against the idea, I was fighting directly against feeding the poor. So it looked like I had to be pumped. I turned to Mike and slapped him on the back. "Pumped isn't even the word," I said.

The game was on.

One night in the midst of all this, I came home and found my mom was there early. "Hi, San!" she said brightly. "You'll never guess who called today."

"Uh, the Pope? The Dalai Lama? Aunt Marlene?"

"None of the above. It was your friend's mom."

"Which friend?" Yeah, like I had so many.

"You know, the girl you're always with. The one

with the 1950s Boy Scout name — Chippy? Gopher? Spanky?"

"Her name's Woody, Mom."

"I know. It's just so hard to keep track of the names of people I've *never even met*. Anyway, her mom told me she'd been hoping to get to know me. She asked if I was going to the big game. I said, what big game? She just laughed, like I had to be kidding. So I have a date with Jippy's mom to see some basketball thing at your school next week. Isn't that exciting?"

"Exciting isn't even the word," I choked out.

"Will Lippy be there, do you think? Apparently she arranged this whole event. She must be some girl! Well, I always figured that when my Sanny fell in love and completely hid it from his mother, the girl who stole his heart would have to be pretty special."

She looked at me with that look moms have, like *I dare you to deny what I just said*. But I wouldn't crack. The stakes were too high. She sighed and then gave a little laugh. "The funniest part, though, is what her mom said when I first got the phone. She said, 'You don't sound like I'd imagined you would.' What did you tell these people about little old me, San? I just *wonder* about that."

She glared some more. But I was unbreakable. "Well, Sanny, I guess the whole Woody family will get to find out exactly what I'm like at the game next Tuesday. Won't it be wonderful when I go to your school and meet all the interesting new people in your life? I can't wait! It should be very . . . educational for me."

And for some other people too, I thought.

This was starting to remind me way too much of the day my dad's lies had started unraveling. We were in Houston, and I thought things were going great. But out of the blue, Dad sat down at breakfast and announced that we'd be moving in a few weeks. My mom didn't even bother to ask why. I'd never asked why before either, but this time I needed to. I had done a poster project on the ancient Incas for Mrs. Brown's social studies class, and I was supposed to present it at a history fair the next month. I had never been honored by anyone before, for anything, and I had a weird feeling that Mrs. Brown really cared about me. Dad was always saying not to get too attached to people — which was actually very Zen of him but for totally wrong reasons. Still, I'd let myself get attached to this lady, and I didn't want to let her down.

Can you believe it? My dad was in jail because I'd gotten carried away with some Sharpies and glitter glue.

But I'm getting ahead of the story. I asked my dad why we were always moving, and he said, "I'm your father, and I know what's best for this family."

Maybe it was just too early in the morning for me to think clearly, or maybe I was temporarily insane, because I shot back, "That's not an answer to my question."

"You have to trust me, San."

"You always tell me I should never trust anyone, Dad."

As Mom gave my hand a little warning squeeze under the table, Dad said, "San, I'm telling you, there are reasons why we can't stay too long, opportunities I don't want us to miss out on."

"Opportunities? What about the opportunity for me to be a normal kid? What about the opportunity to stay in one school for more than a year? What about the opportunity to be part of a community? My social studies teacher says that —"

"Your SOCIAL STUDIES TEACHER? Is he putting these crazy ideas in your head? That you should disrespect your elders? That you should defy your own father?"

"She, Dad. My social studies teacher is a she. Which you would know if you ever bothered to listen to your only son instead of spending all your time gambling on the Internet when Mom's not —"

POW! Not for the first time, my father knocked me out of my chair. But for the first time, he left a visible mark — when I saw the fist coming at my shoulder, I had turned to avoid it, but in the wrong direction. I pushed myself up from the floor, bolted out the door before he could stop me, and ran all the way to school. I didn't know what to do when I got there; I just knew I couldn't make it through the day, much less another move. Like a zombie, I shuffled upstairs and somehow found my way to Mrs. Brown's room. She was sitting at her big old-fashioned wooden teacher desk drinking coffee, and when she looked up at me she spilled about half the cup on the floor. She asked what had happened to my eye and I couldn't talk. I couldn't say anything. I was just crying and crying until I couldn't even breathe.

The next thing I remember, I was in the counselor's office with Mrs. Brown and a lady from the Texas Department of Child Welfare. The lady wanted to talk to me alone, but Mrs. Brown refused to leave. When the woman finally gave in and let Mrs. Brown stay, I decided to talk.

You know what's funny? According to the child welfare office, the one black eye I was sporting wasn't enough to prove what they called a "persistent pattern of abuse." And in some technical sense they were right: Dad only hit me maybe once or twice a year, but that was only because I was usually so good at staying out of his way. So Dad would have gotten away with the whole thing. But apparently when they ran his name through their computer, they came up with warrants from California. And Alabama. And Connecticut.

You know the rest. My dad's last lesson to me was that it's always the random little stuff that gets you busted. Like a charity basketball game, for example.

Slam, dunk, crack —
part one

So the tide of karma rolled over me, and I had no choice but to flow with it. If my mom was going to meet Woody's mom, and Woody was going to hate me forever for being a liar, and my favorite pet basketball team was lining up to get slaughtered, I could at least do my best to make the game interesting.

I called the B team eighth graders together in gym a week before the game and asked about their practice schedule. It turned out that both they and the A team had their practices cancelled for the week by the basketball coach, who had said each team should practice by itself at least twice before the game. I told the guys I thought we should practice every day except Wednesday, because of the soup kitchen. Mike turned to me. "We?" he asked. "Does that mean you'll help us after school too?"

It just amazed me that these people still thought I was helping them get better at basketball. All I did was make up crazy psychological stuff to do with them, and then call it Zen. On the other hand, the game was in seven days, and no traditional method was going to put the team on top in that amount of time. So I decided to go full Ninja with this thing. I pulled Woody aside and told her my plan. Then we got the boys in a huddle.

That week we had some crazy practices. Tuesday was "Dodgeball Drill Day." The team did all of its usual practice drills — which were totally mystifying to me — but with an added twist: Woody and I ran up and down the sidelines lobbing big red rubber dodgeballs at them randomly in the middle of each play. Thursday was "Laser Tag Fest"; Woody borrowed some ancient, dusty laser tag vests and guns from the gym department. The players wore the vests, and Woody and I shot at whoever had the ball throughout the practice. The rule was that if the ball carrier got hit, he had to pass the ball at that very second. Friday was "Water Balloon Follies" on the outdoor court: nothing but shooting drills, and if a player missed three times — *SPLOOSH!* Good thing it was a lovely, warm fifty-two degrees that day.

Saturday and Sunday were three-on-three games at the outside court, but Sunday's game was on roller skates. On Monday, the last practice before the game, we played indoor court hockey and soccer instead of basketball. At the very end of the workout, Mike got everyone together and gave a pretty inspiring little speech. His theme? *B is for Brotherhood*. I didn't point out that B is also for *Bison*. Then Woody said a few words too, about pulling together, but also about having fun and remembering that the game was a fund-raiser, not a blood match. Finally everyone looked at me. I stood at the center of the team, at the center of the court, looked each member right in the eye, and nodded at them in turn.

Mike said, "That's it? Just a bunch of nods? Don't you have anything for us?"

I thought for a minute. "All right, Michael, I give you each two strong legs."

"We already have those."

"OK, I give each of you two strong arms."

"We have those too. I mean, can't you give us anything that we don't already have?"

I smiled. "No. I can't give you anything you don't already have. You don't need anything else." I bowed to him, and then he smiled too. I started to walk away. Woody called me back and dragged a big box out from behind the bleachers. "San, I have a surprise for you. We made T-shirts for tomorrow. They'll be our uniforms, and we're going to sell them to the crowd too. I think we'll make at least another few hundred bucks for the soup kitchen with these." She reached into the box. "Here's yours."

I looked for a long moment as she held up a black shirt, and then turned it around. The front said GOT ZEN? under a yin–yang. The back had a picture of a guy shooting a bow and cracking up at the same time. I frowned, and Woody must have thought I was missing the meaning.

"See, San? It's a laughing archer — you know, like the words on your notebook. We thought your mysterious name might give us luck. So that's the name of our team: The Laughing Archers. Catchy, right?"

"Wait, Woody. You guys don't actually, uh, believe all that stuff Peter's been saying about The Laughing

Archer, do you? The whole seventh coming of Buddha thing? Signs and wonders?"

They all gave each other quick little glances of embarrassment. Mike piped up, "No, San, of course not," which led to a whole chorus of denials. But just from their sheepishness, I got the shocking feeling they sort of believed it. Mike locked eyes with me. "That's just kind of a joke, right?" he asked.

I looked down at myself: the stained, sweaty gym shirt; the shorts so big I could have shared them with a friend; the cracked and peeling sandals. I wanted to shout, *Are you freakin' KIDDING me? Could I look LESS dignified without, say, wearing a chicken on my head? If I'm a reincarnated god, then Mr. Dowd is secretly Britney Spears's love slave.*

But instead I just said, "We're all Buddhas, Michael. All of us."

End of conversation.

End of practice.

Beginning of scary night.

As Woody and I walked out of the gym, I thought, *This is probably the last time she'll ever want to be anywhere near me. After tomorrow, it will be all over.* So, of course she looked more beautiful to me than ever before. I wanted to reach out and push the hair out of her eyes so gently that she would swoon. Admittedly I was a little unclear on how exactly one swoons, or even whether I'd be able to tell she was doing it, but I assumed swooning was better than hating me like she would after the game. I almost stopped her on the steps of the school, led her to our rock, and told her everything. Really I did. But when we got out there, Peter was waiting for her.

"Hi, Emily," he said as he smirked relentlessly. "Mom didn't want you walking alone with the Meditating Molester here, so she sent me to escort you. Even though I told her the Buddha Boy was too removed from earthly desires to make a move on you, she just wouldn't take no for an answer. Sorry, San. I guess you'll just have to laugh and arch yourself home without my sister."

"No problem. We live in different directions anyway. Plus you and Woody should spend more alone

time together. In my culture, family is very important. I will see you tomorrow. Enjoy your time with
your stepsister."

I had to get that "step" part in there. Peter was
gritting his teeth. "You know we're going to kick
your boys' second-rate butts tomorrow, right, San?"

"Well, I should hope so. If the A team didn't beat
the B team, that would really be tremendously
embarrassing. Wouldn't it, Woody?"

Behind Peter's back, she was almost laughing. I
took a second to enjoy that face. Then I fired my
parting shot. "But Peter? Isn't Michael one of your
best friends? Should you really be so gleeful about
kicking his second-rate butt? In a charity game?
Please think about it, all right?"

Heh-heh. Let him chew on that for a while.

While I went home and chewed on my nerves. What
was going to happen when my mom met Woody's
mom? I mean, I could probably have made up some
lie to explain Mom's undeniable non-Asian-ness, but
the cat would be out of the bag as soon as they

started talking anyway. Was there some desperate, last-minute plan that could get me out of this? Could I pretend I was deathly ill and skip the whole event? I knew that some guys had gotten out of serving in the Vietnam War by shooting themselves in the foot. Maybe I could slam my toes in my bedroom door or something, and then — and then nothing. I would just be forced to attend the game on crutches, and that wouldn't stop the dreaded Meeting of the Moms. My only chance was to get struck by lightning on the way to school in the morning. Maybe if I con-structed a special electro-attraction suit out of tinfoil and clothes hangers, I could manage to get myself fried in time — IF it happened to be raining.

Oh, who was I kidding? This was my last night of happiness, for sure. Well, except for the fact that I was already miserable. Dang.

At dinner, Mom felt like talking. I didn't. She gave up. I went to my room and stared around at every-thing, like a caged animal. Then I had a strange thought: What if I actually sat and meditated? Like for real, to calm myself down. So I tried it. And it worked great. After about half an hour of sitting zazen, I was much more at peace about this. I even resolved to tell Woody the whole truth myself in the morning, and face whatever came.

Naturally, after a good night's sleep, I came to my senses and reminded myself that I was a total coward who loathed confrontations of any kind. So when I arrived at school in my cool new Laughing Archers T-shirt, all I did was talk with Woody about her biological-mom situation. She still hadn't heard from her mother after sending the recording, but said she was feeling OK with the whole deal. I think her exact words were, "I gave it my best shot. At least now if I don't hear back, I'll always have that." I was thinking, *Yeah, it must be nice to have guts. Not that I'd know from personal experience, though.*

School happened with all its usual breathtaking excitement and beauty. The high point, as always, was lunch. Woody was playing a brand-new song. I mean, it was a seventy-year-old song by Woody Guthrie, but it was brand-new to me. The words were really appropriate:

It's a hard and it's hard, ain't it hard
To love one that never did love you.
It's a hard and it's hard, ain't it hard, great God,
To love one that never will be true?

I haven't really talked about Woody's voice yet, and I guess I should. Listening to her, most of the time, was like hearing water bubbling and flowing over smooth stones. Her voice was just that natural and easy. Me, I trip if I try to pace while I'm on the phone. But Woody could play these amazing little runs on the guitar while she sang a totally different melody, and it came floating out of her like she was born to sing just that one song, at just that one moment. Woody sang so well that you almost forgot she was singing, if that makes any sense.

But on this one song, there was a jagged angle to her tone, like the words were being ripped out of her one by one. When the song was over, it looked like she might have been crying a little. I just wanted to put my Cheesy Mac platter aside, run to her, and let her bury her face in my shoulder. But I didn't.

Stupid me.

The rest of the day dragged, but eventually school was over, and it was time for the basketball game. I felt my heart hammering away as I walked down the hall to the gym with Woody. On the outside, I was this calm guy, smoothly complimenting Woody on her singing, and chatting about hoops strategy. On the inside, I was dying piece by piece as I thought, *This is it, my good-bye walk with the girl of my dreams. I have to remember everything — how she looks at this exact second, the way the Laughing Archer shirt matches the little black rubber bracelet she's twisting as we talk, the way I feel when we're washing dishes together. And then I have to say so long to all of it.*

I went into the locker room, and Woody went into the gym to make sure the T-shirts were getting sold and the ticket money was being collected. I don't know how she and the team had set every-thing up without my noticing, but then again, even

Zen masters can't concentrate on everything at once. Whatever. The B team and A team were at totally opposite ends of the changing area. The A team had the prime location right near the showers, which put them closest to me, right behind a partition, as I walked in. I overheard an interesting little convo between Peter and some guy with a squeaky voice.

Peter: Let's go, guys. We have to crush them today!

Squeak: Uh, chill, Pete. It's just for fun, right?

Peter: No, it's not for fun. This is for our reputation! It's for our names and our honor.

Squeak: No, it's not. It's to get ready for the spring tournaments and raise money to feed poor people.

Peter: What kind of attitude is that?

Squeak: What, wanting to have fun playing against my friends and feed the poor? I guess you're right, Jones. I have an attitude problem.

I walked away smiling, and went to give some last-minute nuggets of wisdom to my team. In fact (and I'm not proud of this), I had memorized a famous Zen speech about sword fighting and adapted it to basketball. I got the guys in a semicircle around me and gave my stolen pep talk: "If you place your mind on your opponent's ball handling, your mind is absorbed by your opponent's ball handling. If your mind is on your opponent's passing, your mind is absorbed by your opponent's passing. If your mind is on your opponent's shooting, your mind is absorbed by your opponent's shooting. If your mind is on your dribbling, your mind will be absorbed by your dribbling. If your mind is on your passing, your mind will be absorbed by your passing. If your mind is on your shooting, your mind will be absorbed by your shooting. And don't even get me started on rebounds.

"My point is, there is nowhere to put your mind. You need to be mindless out there."

"Hey, no fair," somebody yelled out, "Mike has an unfair advantage!"

They all laughed, but then they all looked back at me blankly. Mike spoke up. "Um, San? What does all that stuff have to do with basketball? Are you telling us to just kinda shut up and play?"

I smiled. "Yes, Michael. Shut up and play."

We hit the court. I spaced out during the pregame rituals, which Woody handled, because they were totally baffling to me anyway, and found myself searching the bleachers for signs of my mom. I saw Woody's stepmother, but she was sitting with a man. I had a glimmer of hope: Maybe my mom was stuck in a massive traffic jam. Or maybe she had gotten hung up in surgery at the hospital. Or maybe the game was sold out and she couldn't get in.

Except there were no traffic jams in our little suburb, my mom wasn't a surgical nurse, and even though the crowd was bigger than I would have liked, there were still tons of empty spaces in the bleachers. Hmm . . . maybe Woody's stepmom had dumped my mother so she could have a hot date. Woody came back to our bench from the middle of the court, leaned over to me, and whispered, "My dad is here!" That explained the hot date, but not where my mom was.

I temporarily forgot all about searching the stands when the game began. Instead, I spent the first half watching my Laughing Archers turn into Limping Losers. Woody handled all the substitutions and stuff (not that there was a lot of subbing to do, because we only had one spare guy), so all I had to do was sit and cringe as the A team built up a fifteen-point lead. They were faster than us, taller, stronger. Plus they had all these cool passing plays worked out that left our defense helpless. The worst part was Peter. Nobody else on the court was playing a particularly physical game, but he sure was — at the half he had two personal fouls, and one of our guys had to come out of the game with a bloody nose after Peter spiked a blocked shot back in his face. Peter also had seventeen of his team's thirty-two points. Woody's dad was cheering for him like crazy too. I wondered if Woody was noticing and if it was hurting her feelings. I didn't get the chance to ask her before the half, though, because she was prowling the sideline nonstop, shouting basketball-expert-type orders at our team, and yelling advice to the referees too. I was out of my element, but Peter and Woody were definitely immersed in theirs. The only good news for me was that we were seven-for-seven on free throws.

At halftime, nobody even bothered to speak to me. I patted them on the back, threw them towels, and refilled their water cups — but this was now Woody's show. Maybe we should have called the team The Fighting Singers or something, because Woody was riled up: "That was not acceptable, gentlemen. They're making you look like — like —"

"The B team?" Mike offered.

"Yeah, the B team."

"But we are the B team, Woody."

"Not today, you're not. Today you're The Laughing Archers, and that means you're not going to go back out there and lose."

"Um, I thought in the Zen religion winning wasn't the point."

Woody almost snarled at him. "Well, Mike, I'm

Catholic. And I want to see those arrogant dorks over there go *down*. Here's the plan. You're not going to contain my brother with a straight zone defense; if we go man-to-man, they're better than us one-on-one, and double-teaming my brother will make it even worse."

"Wow, Woody, you're a real beacon of hope."

"Shut up, Mike. If zone doesn't work and man doesn't work, we have to think outside of the box. You know the triangle offense? Well, we're going to go with a sort of inverted triangle defense. Mike, you'll still cover my brother, but everyone else needs to be more flexible. You know that little, fast guard, Steve Winn?"

That had to be the guy with the squeaky voice.

"Yeah? What about him?"

"Well, we're not going to cover him at all unless he's in the paint. He's too quick for any of you anyway. And we're not going to cover Craig What's-his-name if he gets in the paint — he has no inside shot. So when they're bringing the ball up, Steve's guy is going to break off and cover about five feet behind whoever's defending Peter. If Steve gets in close, his defender will switch back to him, and Craig's guy will stay between Peter and the basket. It will be like a very soft double-team — much harder for Peter than just one of you guys being on him, but harder on the rest of their offense than a straight double-team. Got it?"

"Uh, sure. Got it, guys?"

They all mumbled what sounded like the word *yes* would sound if you inflected it as a *maybe*. Then Mike said, "What about offense, Woody?"

"Definitely, we should try having some. And by the way, you're playing like little girls out there — Peter's pounding on you. Where's your aggression? Where's your drive? Where are your freaking ELBOWS? God gave them to you for a reason — so you could throw them around on the court." She peered over at me.

"Do you have anything to add, San?"

"Uhh — go, team?"

She rolled her eyes, and a ref blew a whistle. It was time to start playing Woody's game. And we did. Sure, our guys started getting called for fouls — but their guys hadn't been practicing their foul shots like we had. And as their other players started to join Peter's parade of fouls, we started catching up. Whatever Woody's weird defense triangle thing meant, it was working great too — Peter was getting all frustrated, and their other players weren't scoring enough to make up the difference. All of a sudden we were within five points of them.

Then two things happened at once: I saw my mom walk in, and Mike got mad at Peter.

Slam, dunk, crack —
part two

Yikes!

I looked up from the game for a moment, and there she was, wearing a bright red scarf. She was looking around the crowd, as if she was trying to find someone. I followed the angle of her head; she was staring at little sixth-grade Justin, my rock-sitting buddy, who was holding a huge posterboard with the words SAN FAN written on it in fluorescent marker. Mom shook her head and started scanning the bleachers some more. I wondered how she expected to pick out Woody's parents if she had never met them before. There must have been some kind of confusion, because she just kept standing in the doorway instead of going to a seat.

A whistle brought my attention back to the action on the court. Mike and Peter were up in each other's faces, and the refs were trying to get between them. Mike was shouting at the officials, "Didn't you see that? He fouled me! That's three personals. Kick him out!"

But the officials hadn't seen whatever Peter had done. Thanks to my mom's entrance, neither had I. Woody went out to argue, and I ran over to get Mike away from Peter. I actually managed to drag him about ten feet backward, but then he yelled over my shoulder at the refs, "What are you, blind? Jesus!"

They kicked him out of the game. We were in trouble here. The nosebleed kid was in no shape to get back in and play, so, with no Mike, we were down to four players. Woody came up to me and said, "San, what are we going to do now?"

"Uh, power play?"

"That's hockey, not basketball. Seriously, what are we going to do? We're almost caught up, and I am *not* going to forfeit."

I said, "What am I supposed to do, magically come up with another player?"

Woody smiled. "San, you're a genius!"

The next thing I knew, I was in uniform. The refs said I couldn't play in sandals, so Mike gave me his damp, sweaty, two-sizes-too-big socks and sneakers to wear. They were so big, I felt like Ronald McDonald out there. And the dampness was no fun either. But there was no choice. I clomped out onto the court, and the whole place started cheering.

Crud. I looked at my mother, still standing in the doorway. She smiled and waved. Then the entire crowd started chanting, "Buddha! Buddha!" And the fun started. The A team guys must have assumed I was some kind of fearsome secret weapon, because they immediately double-teamed me. I'd like to say that my fleet footwork and slick moves got me into the clear over and over, that then I unleashed a devastating barrage of baskets, that I was carried off the court a hero. But I didn't have fleet footwork, I didn't get a shot off for the first ten minutes I played, and the only chance I had of getting carried off the court would be on a stretcher.

But the rest of my team started driving to the hoop over and over again while the A team was worrying about guarding me. Before you could say "thinking without thinking," we were only trailing by two points. Peter called a time-out and got his team together.

When they came back on, the double-team was gone, and Peter was defending me. "You've got nothing, San," he growled as he bumped into my chest.

"True," I said. "I'm surprised it took you a period to figure that out, though."

While he was trying to come up with a witty reply, we scored again. The game was all tied up!

On our next possession, we missed. Then they got off a lucky three-pointer, putting their team up by three with less than a minute left in the game. Woody was shouting, "Fast break! Fast break!" We charged up the court, but I was tripping over the tips of Mike's huge shoes, so I was way behind everybody else. One of our guys went up for the world's easiest layup and missed. But he threw the ball so hard off the rim that it flew over everyone's heads and into my waiting hands. Peter was running too fast to turn around in time, so I was all alone at the three-point line for a split second. I was afraid of what would happen if I gave Peter time to guard me, so I shot without thinking. Peter had swung his arm around to block the ball, and his fingers slammed into my chest just after I released the shot. The ref's whistle blew, the buzzer went off to end the game, and my shot went in.

Swish.

I came down and fell on top of Peter. It was a total accident, but a very hard impact. My knees slammed into the tops of his legs, and his head smashed into my ribs. We landed in a heap. I couldn't move, because I couldn't breathe — Peter's fingers had knocked half of the wind out of me, and his skull finished the job. Peter was under me, writhing in pain. "Get the hell off me, Buddha!" he gasped as he rolled over and tumbled me onto the floor.

I lay there trying to fill up my screaming lungs, while Peter sat up next to me, clutching one hand with the other. Somebody grabbed me from behind and helped me up. Then the ref handed me the ball. We were all tied up, the clock had run out, and I had one foul shot.

This was unbe-freakin'-lievable.

I staggered to the line. Peter stood right next to me. The whole gym was silent, so it was easy for me to make out what he grunted at me as I bent my knees. "You've still got nothing, Buddha."

"Except your sister," I said as I unleashed my best shot.

return to
sender

The next morning on my rock I thought about how strange life is. What were the chances that my worst nightmare would have turned into a glorious dream? I was a temporary basketball star, my mom and Woody's family hadn't met, and I had one last chance to make things right with Woody.

Can you believe Peter broke a finger against my chest? During the chaos after my foul shot won us the game, Woody's dad came bounding onto the court, took one look at Peter's right pinky, and whisked the whole family off to the emergency room. Peter had only had enough time to give me the threatening glare of a lifetime before Woody's hair blocked my view of him. My mom had come down onto the court too — just in time to see the Long/Jones clan hustling out the exit door.

"Was that your friend Winky?" she asked.

"Yes, Mom, that *was* Woody."

"Where's she going? Were those her parents?

Who's that horrible boy who kept banging into you? And where did you learn to shoot like that?"

"She's going to the hospital. Yes, those are her parents. Her dad thinks her brother — the horrible boy — broke a bone on the last play of the game. And I don't know how to shoot; that was just luck."

"Some luck. Speaking of which, I had none at all meeting up with Woody's mother. I told her I'd be wearing a bright red scarf, and she said she'd have no trouble spotting me. Her eyes must not be as great as she thinks they are."

"I'm sorry about that, Mom. Did you like the game?"

"Yes, although I don't know why you had to borrow some boy's sneakers when you have perfectly nice ones of your own."

"Well, I like wearing my sandals, especially now that spring is here. You know, that's why I stopped wearing my winter coat for the year too."

"I wouldn't count on the weather staying like this, Sanny. You know, my favorite poet, T. S. Eliot, said that April is the cruelest month."

Wow, my mom had a favorite poet. Who knew?

Woody snapped me back to the present with her usual gentle morning greeting: "San, you wouldn't believe what a pathetic FIASCO my night was! I hate the world, I really do."

So much for my confession. "What's wrong, Woody?"

"Well, first of all, Peter's finger is broken. So he's out today to get this huge cast put on, and he won't be able to play in the varsity tournament next week. He's really upset, and he's blaming the whole thing on you."

"Uh, he already hates me anyway, right? So don't worry about it."

"San, I think he might try to start a fight with you."

"With his finger broken?"

"I don't know, he's pretty mad. And I'm afraid you'll hurt him."

I started to protest, like, *Hello? Have you seen the size of your brother?* But Woody wasn't done talking. "San, please promise me you won't hurt him."

What did she think I was — some kind of fighting Samurai? Did I look tough? I swear, I've seen rubber duckies more menacing than I am. Sheesh! Plus, the

Samurai were Japanese, anyway. "Um, OK, Woody. If it comes to a fight, I promise I won't hurt him *too* badly."

She looked relieved. She actually looked *relieved* that I wasn't going to use my head to pummel her stepbrother's precious little ham-sized fists. But she wasn't done with her list of problems. "There's another thing too, San."

"I'm listening."

"When we got home yesterday, the mail was there."

She stopped talking and her face broke. She tried several times to keep talking, but I couldn't understand her through the wave of sobs. I put my arms around her and she cried into my shirt. It was a weird feeling.

When she finally got her voice working again, she said, "The package came back, San. There was a big red stamp on it: return to sender, no such addressee. She moved. She moved without letting us know. She's really . . ." Her voice started to crumble again, but she swallowed a few times and reined it in. "She's really gone."

I just held Woody and stroked her hair, because really, what do you say to make *that* better?

"I mean, I knew she wasn't coming back. I *knew* she didn't love me enough. But I still kind of believed."

I felt her body stiffening against mine. I pulled my head back and saw that now she looked mad. "I was an idiot, San. I was so stupid. Well, I'll tell you this: Nobody's ever going to fool me again."

Oh, swell.

"And another thing: I'll never play another Woody Freaking Guthrie song again as long as I live. Never!"

"But you worked so hard to learn all those songs."

"For *her*!" Woody was so angry that I could feel her shudder as she said the word *her*. Well, this was a fun sneak preview of my future.

"But it was for you too. You know, I actually wrote about you and your mom on my English essay test."

"You *what?*"

"I wrote about you. Look, you know the whole middle path thing?"

"Yeah."

"Well, the way I see it, when you were playing nothing but songs your mom liked, you were letting her control you."

She stamped her foot and spat, "I know! That's why I'm finished with those songs."

"But then she's still controlling you."

"What are you talking about? From now on, I'm doing the exact opposite of what she would want."

"Right, which means she's still controlling you. As long as it's all or nothing, your mom is still defining your choices. And who says you have to be just one thing anyway?"

"So what am I supposed to do, play half Woody Guthrie and half My Chemical Romance? What do you call that — Hobo-Emo? Folk-core?"

"I can't tell you what to play or what to call it."

"So what do I play then?"

I looked at her. She looked at me. "Play what you feel like playing, Woody. That's all."

She pouted as she murmured, "Easy for you to say. You know exactly who you are." But she put her head against my chest. It kind of ached because her forehead was leaning right on the huge bruise her brother had given me. But truthfully, I think even without the bruise, it would have ached anyway.

As the school bell rang, Woody asked, "So did my problems get you an A, at least?"

"I got a B+ on the test. I missed a couple on the multiple-choice part. But she wrote, 'Very honest and insightful' under the essay about you."

She grabbed both of my hands and squeezed them. "That's my San."

Inside the school we got mobbed. The game was the Big News of the Day. Everybody was slapping my back, shaking my hand, rubbing my hair. But I had never felt less like a hero. I faked it all day while everyone on the planet ran up to me to recite little bits of their postgame play-by-play analysis, but Woody's mood and my secrets ruined the whole delusion of popularity for me.

Don't you hate it when your mom is right, by the way? As Woody and I were walking to the soup kitchen that afternoon, it started to snow. This wasn't like a little dinky spring flurry either — in the space of maybe ten minutes, it went from slightly gray and cool to full-out blizzard. Before my dad lost us our computer, I used to be addicted to checking the weather online, so I would have known this was coming. But I had had no warning about this storm. Judging from Woody's wardrobe — a long-sleeved Beatles T-shirt and holey jeans — she had missed the memo too. By the time we got to the shelter, we were totally covered in white. Even Woody's eyebrows were ice-crusted. Normally this would have been the strange kind of fun we both liked, but she was still on a rampage. And like the snow, our problems were going to get a lot deeper.

Stepping into the dishwashing room felt like jumping from a walk-in fridge into a sauna. The snow melted out of my hair so fast that streams ran down my face and neck. The same thing was happening with Woody, except she had a lot more hair, so she was even wetter. She bent over and shook her hair like a dog, which sprayed water all over me. That finally got her smiling. I was smiling too, because every time she looked happy, I got happy. There was nobody around; Mildred, Sister Mary Clare, and the regular helpers were all cooking and serving, and the basketball team had taken the night off. I don't know how it happened — and this isn't just some excuse; I really don't know — but Woody started hugging me. Or I started hugging her, I don't know. It just felt good to have a warm moment in the cold day.

And the next thing I knew, Woody and I were almost kissing. I couldn't let this happen when she didn't know the truth. I held her at arms' length and said, "Woody, wait. This isn't right."

"You mean, because of your whole earthly attachments thing? But we *are* attached, San Lee. Don't you know that? I knew it the first day I ever saw you. Can't you feel it every time we're anywhere near each other?"

If my whole face hadn't already been red from its rapid deicing, it sure would have gotten red in a hurry. "Um, well . . ."

She pulled me closer. "Look at me, San. *Really* look at me. I know you can feel it."

Oh, boy. "But what about the other guy?"

"What other guy?"

"You know, ELL? You write his initials all over your notebooks and everything? I always thought —"

"ELL? ELL? Oh, San. Do you mean that day in social studies when you grabbed that piece of paper to pick up the sand?"

"Yeah, and you got all embarrassed."

"I did get all embarrassed. But ELL isn't another guy. I'm still embarrassed about this. I wrote ELL because I was picturing . . ."

"What, Woody? What were you picturing?"

"My initials. My married initials, I mean. If we ever, uh . . ." She stopped talking and put her head against my chest. What a day my ribs were having!

ELL. Emily Long Lee. I was the biggest fool alive. I felt the mother of all goofy grins starting to burst out on my face. "Oh, Emily," I said into her hair. "All this time I thought . . ."

She put a finger to my lips. "Shh . . ." she murmured.

"Wait, Emily. I still have to tell you something."

"Well, you'd better hurry. A librarian could come bursting in here any minute — or worse, a *nun*! And I don't think we want that."

As it turned out, either of those would have been better than what did happen.

the revenge of
peter jones

OK, I just want to make one point here. I mean, it's important that I emphasize this: I was about to tell her. I was. All right? Even though every nerve cell in my body was screaming *KISS THE GIRL,* I was fighting off the urge so that I could, at long last, fess up. I ran out of time.

Because at that instant, my mom came barging in. Her arms were full of winter clothes. She had my coat, my gloves, and of course my bright red Nike high-tops. Woody looked bewildered, like, *Who's the old chick with the hideous wardrobe?* But unfortunately, her confusion got cleared up real fast when my mom started talking a mile a minute.

"Hi, San. And you must be Woody. It's nice to finally meet you in person. San's told me so much about you! Well, actually, he's told me remarkably little about you — but that tells me a lot anyway. San, I brought your winter clothes. There's about four inches of snow out there already, and it's still coming down like crazy. Didn't I tell you April was the cruelest month?"

She didn't know the half of it. I said, "Thanks, uh, ma'am."

She turned to Woody. "Isn't our boy so polite? You're a lucky girl, Woody. My son might not be the best at introductions, but he's got great manners once you get to know him. Hello. I'm Diane Lee, San's mother."

Woody pushed me away. "*You're* San's mother? And those are San's winter clothes?"

Mom said, "Yes and yes. I'm not surprised you haven't seen the clothes, though. He has this odd habit of shoving them in a sewer pipe every morning."

She *knew* about that? I had to say something, fast. "Uh . . . um . . ." Wow, am I brilliant or what? I guess I won't be a criminal defense lawyer when I grow up.

Woody was looking less puzzled and more upset by the second. "Wait, this is your mom. She's not Chinese. Is your dad Chinese?"

I shook my head.

"So all that stuff about 'your traditions' and 'your culture' was just — what? A total lie? You just completely *made it up?*"

I nodded, just as Mildred and Sister Mary Clare walked in to see what the commotion was.

"And what about your whole Zen thing?"

My mom chimed in, less than helpfully. "Oh, you mean that research project you two are doing? When I first took San to the library, I didn't —"

"THE LIBRARY? SAN LEARNED ALL HIS ZEN STUFF FROM THE LIBRARY?" Woody grabbed my shirt like she was going to hit me. "You're not really a . . . a . . . Zen guy?"

Mildred burst out laughing. "Wait a minute, Emily. You thought San was a real Zen Buddhist? Oh, is that an absolute riot! This boy is about as Zen as Sister Mary here."

Woody *was* going to hit me. Or cry, which would be worse. "San, if you're not really a Buddhist, who are you?"

Mom stepped up to bat for me yet again. I wished she'd been born without a tongue. "Listen, Woody,

San's had a tough year. Ever since his dad went to prison, he's been trying to find himself. I think this Zen thing is just, you know, a phase."

"Your dad's in prison? And this is a phase? Am I a phase too, San? Am I?"

Boy, the dishes were really piling up.

"Hey," I said, "you know, these dishes are really piling up. Do you think we could maybe get back to work? I mean, this is a very interesting conversation and all, but . . ."

Woody ran out of the room crying. My mom dropped all of my garish winter clothes at my feet and followed her. Sister Mary Clare left too, so I was standing there with Mildred, alone. "San, you're a nice boy. I can tell. But what on earth were you thinking, lying to Emily all year? Didn't you know the truth would come out? For goodness' sake, the *essence* of Zen is truth. Maybe I should have given you some philosophy books before the gardening one."

I kicked my clothes aside and started in on the dishes. Mildred rolled up her sleeves and got right to work next to me. "I'm not a nice boy," I said. "I'm a second-generation convict." Then for some reason I told her everything. By the time I was done talking, the dishes were all finished up. I sat on the counter, as usual, and Mildred swung herself up too, with shocking grace. She must have seen my surprise, because she flexed one bicep and said, "Pilates. And calcium tablets. Anyway, San, you *are* a nice boy."

"How can you tell?"

"Library books. You've taken out what, forty books in the past few months? And you've brought them all back in the same condition you got 'em in. That's a sure sign of character. Plus you're a great dishwasher — another sure sign."

"Character? But I just spent twenty minutes telling you what a total liar I am."

"Well, son, I can tell you one thing I've learned: The real liars never own up to what they've done. So right there, you're not as bad as you think you are."

I smiled and started to thank her profusely, but she cut me off. "You're still in big trouble with that girl, though. So you'd better go find her and tell her everything you just told me."

"Do you think it will work? Do you think she'll understand?"

Mildred snickered. "Are you kidding me, San? There's no chance she'll understand."

"But —"

"But you still have to tell her. Now go!"

I went.

But Woody was gone. So was my mom. Sister Mary Clare was standing in the lobby, slowly and laboriously mopping up the slush that had been dragged in and smeared by hundreds of feet. I grabbed an extra mop and started helping. Right when I first started mopping, she said to me, "Your mother went to take Emily home. She told me she might come back for you, if you're lucky."

I kept mopping. Sister Mary Clare kept talking. "Have you spent much time thinking about repentance, Stanley?"

"Listen, I'm not Catholic. And my name is San Lee, NOT Stanley."

She grinned wickedly, if that's an OK description for a nun's facial expression, and said, "Listen, I'm not being a nun right now; I'm being a nosy old lady. And I know your name isn't Stanley. What do you think I am — deaf?"

I kept mopping. You know, it's actually a very strenuous activity. First of all, a big industrial-size mop weighs like thirty pounds when it's full of water, and you have to push it all around and lift it into the bucket-squeezy thing. Then you have to crank the handle of the squeezer really hard to squish the water out of the mop. Next you have to repeat the process until you realize you're weaker than an old lady. An old lady who doesn't particularly shut up.

"Anyway, San, I think you have some major-league repenting to do. Not because your father is in jail, by the way, but because you've hurt people. You can lay down the burden of whatever your father has done — but you have to carry what *you've* done on your shoulders until it's ready to be laid down."

"And how am I supposed to know when that is?"

"When it doesn't hurt anymore to look in the mirror, that's when you'll know."

"And how do I get there?"

"Well, for starters, you finish mopping this floor so an old lady can rest her feet. Then you figure out whom you've hurt, and start trying to make amends."

"What if they don't want to hear it?"

"Doesn't matter. What matters is that at least I tricked you into mopping my floor."

"No, I'm serious. What if they really don't want to hear it?"

"You have to do what's right because it's right, not because somebody's going to give you a gold star at the end."

Just then, I heard a car horn and saw through the subsiding snow flurries that my mom had pulled up outside.

"Uh, Sister, I have to go now. Um, thanks. For talking to me, I mean."

"See you next week, San."

"Will you? Do you still want me here even though I lied to all of you?"

"Did the dishes get clean? Then we still want you. You might be a fake Zen master . . ." She snorted. ". . . but you're a real dishwasher."

My mom wasn't so kind. She reamed me out all the way home, all the way up the stairs, and all the way into my room. Then she stood outside my closed door and reamed me out some more.

The good news was that she liked Woody.

The bad news was that she wasn't currently so fond of me.

Eventually Mom stomped away down the hall, leaving me to stare at my wall and agonize. Who were the people I'd hurt? Woody, sure. My mom, definitely. Peter. Yikes, Peter. I had spent months purposely trying to make him look as dumb as possible just so I could look good. But he was the good guy. He'd been right that I was going to hurt his sister. Well, stepsister, but still. He'd even tried over and over to *make* me make things right. And now because of my big ridiculous pointless scam, he had a broken bone and a grudge.

And then there was one other person to think about: my dad. I didn't really think I'd hurt him much — he was so totally narcissistic that I wasn't sure anyone *mattered* enough to hurt him. But I had still handled his whole prison situation pretty badly. If right actions were always right, whether you got the star at the end or not, then it didn't matter whether my dad was a total jerk. What mattered was that I couldn't be a jerk as a reaction to his jerkhood.

Jerkitude? Jerk-osity?

Anyway, I decided that, as long as I was trapped in my room anyway, I might as well stop ducking my dad, and face this whole deal head-on. So I wrote him a letter. Here's how it started:

Dear Dad,

(Not bad, right? I kept going, since I was on a roll.)

I'm not sure if you know this, because I'm not sure what Mom has told you, but I have been purposely avoiding your phone calls all year. I am still not ready to talk with you, and I don't know that I will ever be. You hurt me, and lied to me, and left me and Mom in a difficult situation. But I think you deserve an explanation. More than that, I deserve the opportunity to explain to you.

What I have learned since we last saw each other (and actually, I just figured a lot of it out right this minute) is that I am really, really angry with you. And instead of expressing my anger to the person who deserves it, I have reacted by lying, and by hurting everyone around me. So I am writing to tell you this: I am washing my hands of lying and anger. They didn't help you, and they won't help me. Maybe you're learning this too since your sentencing. I hope so.

In the meantime, I have a lot to answer for, but I will answer for it — honestly.

Your son,

San

When I was done writing the letter, I snuck out of my room to get an envelope. But I couldn't find one, and realized I didn't know my dad's current address. So I just left the letter on the living room table, right next to where my mother was sleeping in her chair. She didn't have a blanket on or anything, and it was pretty cold in the apartment, so I tiptoed back to my room, got my extra comforter, and tucked it around her.

It felt kind of good to take care of my mom.

The next morning we had a snow delay, so school started two hours late. My mom left for work without saying a word to me, but that was kind of OK. When I sat down to eat breakfast, I found that she had put my letter in an envelope that she'd addressed to my dad. She had also put a hot-pink Post-it note on the outside of the envelope:

SAN —

GLAD YOU WROTE THIS!

So maybe things might be all right on the mom front. Since I had so much extra time before school, I sat on the living room floor in a sunbeam and meditated. Then I had an extra bowl of Cap'n Crunch. It seemed likely that the extra doses of tranquility and sugar might come in handy.

I put on my huge puffy winter coat, the white gloves, and even the red sneakers before I headed out. This was going to be my first nothing-to-hide day. Outside, the sun was blinding and the snow was about five inches deep. I guessed it would melt off pretty fast, but it sure was sparkly while it lasted. I was having fun stomping and kicking my way to school, until I came within sight of my rock. I had been vaguely hoping that maybe Woody was going to be there waiting to talk things out, but she wasn't around. Peter was there instead. He had dusted the snow off of my spot, and was sitting there like he owned the joint. I could have walked right into school and avoided him completely, but if you're going to have a nothing-to-hide day, you can't be running around hiding, can you? I took a deep breath and strode right over in front of Peter.

"Good morning, Peter."

"Good morning, San." Somehow his tone of voice made my name sound like a curse.

"That's a nice cast." It was one of those bright fluorescent green woven-looking ones, and stretched from almost his elbow down across the line of his second knuckles.

"Yeah, I'm really enjoying it. The best part is that since I broke my finger right at the hand joint, my whole wrist has to be immobilized for two months. So I'll miss out on the basketball tournaments and most of baseball season. Isn't that just great?"

"Listen, Peter, I'm sorry that you got hurt because of me. And I'm sorry I hurt your sister."

"You're kidding, right? This is your usual pretend-saint thing, isn't it? You're still showing off for your fans?"

"No, I'm serious. I feel terrible."

"Not as terrible as you're going to feel. You know, Emily cried for like an hour when she got home last night. What were you thinking? Did you really believe you could fool a whole town forever?"

"I don't know, I just —"

"You just what? You just wanted to be a lying criminal like your father?"

Whoa, that was uncalled for. "Woody told you about my dad?"

"No, San. The Internet told me about your dad. I used to be an office monitor, so I know where the home contact cards are. I snuck in early one morning and wrote down all your family information. It's amazing what you can find out if you know how to look. That's how I found out that Laughing Archer is just some band too."

"So why did you tell the whole world that whole seventh Buddha thing?"

"I wanted to make you stop lying. But you can't take a hint. I tried a million ways to get you to fess up, but you're just too much of a psycho."

"I'm a psycho? You stalked me, you dumped snow on my head, you ruined my Zen garden, you narc'ed on me and Woody to your mom, you tried to make a fool of me in basketball, you hit me hard enough to break your bone, you even left those little notes in my locker — but I'm a psycho?"

"A) I didn't leave any notes in your locker, and b) yes, you are a psycho — a second-generation psycho."

I stepped up to him. He didn't back down. As if by magic, a crowd started to form around us. I noticed that, with the usual perfect timing I'd been having, Woody had finally appeared. I remembered I'd promised her I wouldn't hurt him. That was fine, because I'd promised myself I would avoid getting pounded if possible.

"By the way, San, you know what's interesting about this piece of land right here? It's off school property. So when I beat you down, I won't get suspended."

Swell, I thought.

"Peter, this is stupid. I won't hit a guy with a cast."

"Well," Peter said, "I will!" And then he decked me.

San lee:
boy outcast

It's amazing how fast they turn on you. Peter stood over my twitching form for maybe thirty seconds before he started to walk away. As soon as his back was turned, I propped myself up in a half-sitting position so that I could talk to Woody and Mike, along with whoever else wanted to stay and support me. But nobody stayed. Within a minute, I was alone in the snow, with the metallic tang of blood in my mouth. My nose was gushing and felt like someone had been going at it with a ball-peen hammer and chisel. The inside of my cheek was puffing up against my teeth, and my neck hurt from the whiplash effect of Peter's punch. Of course, there were teachers on outside duty across the street, but the shuffling crowd must have blocked their view of my tragic hemorrhaging scene.

I lay back down on my back and considered my options. I could stay put until I froze to death. I could crawl behind my rock and freeze to death, leaving nothing but a bloody snow angel to mark the site of my destruction. I could get to my feet somehow, stagger home, take some Tylenol, apply ice, watch Oprah.

Or I could march right into school and face the music. After all, this was my nothing-to-hide day. I forced myself to my feet, grabbed my backpack, and trudged into the building. I slid my ID through the secretary's window. She handed me a late pass without even looking up, and said, "That's number five for you, Mr. Lee. You will have to stay tomorrow after school for detention." Then she glanced at me — the blood all over my ultra-bright jacket, the swelling face, the pathetic and beaten posture — and yelled for the assistant principal. I spent about fifteen minutes with him in the nurse's office refusing to tell him anything about what had happened, but insisting that whatever *had* occurred had occurred off school property. Then I got sent to class.

Have you ever been your school's Loser of the Day? It's not like they put your name on the marquee or announce it over the intercom or anything. But everyone in the joint knows exactly who you are and what you've done by the end of homeroom — by first period, at the latest. So you walk through the halls and this little corridor of silence opens up in front of you, while a murmuring cone of scorn fills itself in behind you. Well, at least it was a shortened day, I thought optimistically. I didn't speak to a single soul until social studies ended — athough one kid I'd never met walked up to me, checked out my nose, and said, "Daaaaamn, San," before continuing on his way. I spent Dowd's whole class period trying to get Woody to look at me, but her eyes never wavered from the video we were watching about medieval Europe. I hadn't known she was so fascinated by the feudal system.

When the bell rang, I was ready to bolt out of school before the hallway crowds could slow me down. But Dowd asked me to stay after. I heard various people snickering under their breath, and then the room was empty, except for me and my teacher. "San," he said.

I waited.

"San, San, San."

I felt like belting out, — *TA CLAUS, HERE COMES SANTA CLAUS, RIGHT DOWN SANTA CLAUS LANE.* But the moment didn't seem quite right. Plus my mouth hurt.

"Yes, sir?"

"Sometimes life gets bumpy, doesn't it?"

"Uh, well, in this case, it's just my face that got bumpy."

"I'm glad you can see some small humor in your situation. You know, when a new student moves into my class, especially one with so much ability and promise, I always try to provide support and, well, guidance. But I'm afraid I failed you, San. Did you know that I usually choose my students' project partners randomly, with straws? But just to make you feel more comfortable, I chose by alphabetical order this time around. I thought you would have a better experience if you were assigned to someone helpful and friendly, like Emily Long. I also left several notes in your locker in the hopes that you would give up this little Zen deception of yours. But I suppose things spiraled out of control pretty quickly."

Dowd had left the notes in my locker? "Yeah, I suppose so."

"You know, San, I really have been deeply impressed with your knowledge of Buddhism, and Zen Buddhism in particular. I haven't mentioned this in class, but Zen is of great personal interest to me. I spent several years in Japan during the 1970s. I was in the Army, and there was a Zen monastery right next to the base. I used to go there and meditate with the monks. When I came back to the States and started teaching, I got my sister interested in Zen too. And now she's way ahead of me, I'm afraid."

"Your sister?"

"You know, Mildred."

"Mrs. Romberger is your sister?"

"Why, yes. Hasn't she ever told you that? That's how I knew you were working so hard on your research all year — she is really impressed with you. It's also how I know what happened with you last night. San, what are you going to do now that your cover is, as they say, blown?"

"I don't know, Mr. Dowd. I'm just going to try to

be honest, I guess. And I'll try to be wiser about things."

"Wiser? But after all the studying time you've put in the last few months, aren't you wise already?"

"Mr. Dowd, no offense, but I think I know less now than I did when I started."

His eyes lit up with the full power of the famous Dowd twinkle. "Then you're wiser than you think. Now get out of here. Go home! By the way, you might want to put some ice on that nose before you go to bed tonight."

I got out of there. I went home. And Dowd was right: I did want to put some ice on my nose. Mom flipped when she saw it, and I responded by telling her the truth about how the whole thing had happened. Which led to a lot of other confessions from me. Yikes! It was almost like Sister Mary Clare, in one mopping session, had somehow turned me Catholic. But really, this was just me catching up on a season's worth of honesty.

It felt kind of good.

The next several weeks at school were hard.

Spring came roaring back, and every day was beautiful — which somehow made my outcast status even more painful. I'd be looking out the window in Dowd's class, and there would be bluebirds singing on every branch of the tree over my rock. So I'd almost start feeling cheerful. But when I looked around the room, Woody would be totally ignoring me. Even Peter was pretending I didn't exist.

If I were them, I wouldn't forgive me either.

But as the weeks dragged on toward eighth grade graduation, my outsider status did allow me to observe some very interesting things. I sometimes had the feeling that I had started a wave. The wave had broken over me, but was still rolling, and carrying other people along. A few scenes:

It's English class. We're picking up with Henry David Thoreau again; English Teacher still has her little social studies tie-in going on. She writes a Thoreau quote on the board: "The squirrel that you kill in jest, dies in earnest." A tiny, quiet girl who's also in my Dowd class says, "I know what that means! It means that we should respect every life the way we respect our own. Like the other day, there was this huge stink bug in my kitchen. My mom wanted to smush it, but I caught it and let it go outside." A lot of kids say, "Eww! Gross!" But English Teacher smiles.

It's gym. We're outside playing baseball. Mike is trying to teach some really spastic kid how to pitch. The kid says, "I suck at this. I couldn't throw a strike if home plate was ten feet wide." Mike says, "Form is all that matters." The kid says, "What are you talking about? That's the stupidest thing I've ever heard." Mike grabs the ball out of his hand, steps on the mound, winds up, turns, and hurls it about a mile into the stands. The kid is standing there, speechless, as Mike says, "Who cares where the ball goes?"

It's lunch. Woody sits down with her guitar in her usual spot by the food line. The guitar looks different somehow. It hits me: The Woody Guthrie words have been removed. She plays the Beatles song "With a Little Help from My Friends." People are murmuring and looking over at her when the music ends. She smiles, nods, and breaks into a Nirvana tune called "All Apologies." After that, people start applauding.

She nods again, and strums the beginning to Green Day's "Time of Your Life (Good Riddance)." At the end of that one, someone shouts out, "GO, WOODY!" She yells back, "My name is Emily." Then she starts playing "Hard Travelin'," and looks in my general direction. Not right at me, but it's a start.

Maybe.

It's after school, about three days before graduation. Little Justin is sitting on my rock with his legs crossed. A spunky-looking girl with spiked hair climbs up and sits next to him. They look at each other like they're alone together on an island paradise somewhere. I wish them luck. I know how hard it is to keep one of those things afloat.

It's graduation rehearsal. We're walking in two by two, like animals on Noah's Ark. My usual partner is absent, so the girl behind her steps up. Surprise! It's Woody — as if I haven't been trying all week not to look back at her when we're in line, and across at her when we're in our seats. A teacher stops us suddenly, and I bump elbows with her. Instinctively,

I say, "Excuse me." She looks right in my eyes and says, "Not yet."

It's graduation day, my last time at my locker. I spin the combo, take the lock off, put it in my backpack. I grab out what's left in the locker: my English journal, a half-empty pack of gum. Then I see a scrap of paper sticking partway out of one of the little vent slits in the door. It's one last note from Dowd:

WHEN THE WAY COMES TO AN END, THEN CHANGE — HAVING CHANGED, YOU PASS THROUGH.

I CHING

Underneath the quote, there's a handwritten message. All it says is, "Go see my sister."

I do.

wash your bowl
some more

It's summertime, evening. I'm working alone washing dishes at the soup kitchen. I've been doing this three nights a week since school let out. I've also been volunteering at the library every weekday. Mildred hooked me up. And they're even going to start paying me once school starts. Mom is pretty psyched.

Oh, I forgot to tell you: It's Wednesday. I'm about a third of the way through the meal, and the trays are stacking up. I've gotten faster at this than I could have imagined, but still, some help would be nice. Out of the blue, Woody is next to me. She's wearing jeans shorts and a gray shirt that matches her eyes. She's beautiful. I mean, she's still beautiful. She's always beautiful.

For what seems like an hour, Woody looks at me and I look at her. I can't read her expression at all. Is she furious? Ecstatic? Madly in love with me? I have no clue. I just know I want everything to be right again. No, not again — things were never truly right before, but I want to do everything right from now on.

Clang! The stalemate is broken by commotion as a tray full of silverware slams into the end of the conveyor belt. Woody says, "Move over," and starts pulling on a pair of rubber gloves.

I say, "Listen, I didn't mean to —"

"Shut up."

"No, I mean, I never thought I'd —"

"Hush."

"Emily," I say. "Emily, I'm sorry."

"I know. Now move over."

And just like that we're dish partners again.

When the last tray is drying and we're up on our old counter, I turn to her and say, "I really am sorry. But I've changed. I swear."

She slides sideways until our hips are touching. "Are you? Have you? Do you?"

"I am. I have. I do."

"Good. Now, about those earthly attachments . . ."

having changed,
you pass through

It's the end of the summer, and I'm brushing my teeth before bed, looking in the mirror. High school starts tomorrow. Yikes! High school. I don't know what classes I'll like. I don't know what clubs I'll join (although I'm thinking I might go out for basketball). I only know one person I'll be hanging out with. But maybe that's enough. I really think I'll be OK.

No, I know I'll be OK.

Trust me.

a quick word from the author:

If you are interested in learning more about the theory and practice of Zen, you might want to start where I did, with a charming book called *The Little Zen Companion,* by David Schiller. Many of the quotations in my book may be found collected in Mr. Schiller's fascinating work. Of course you can't really become a Zen practitioner by reading a book, but reading up on the subject will certainly give you a lot of food for thought.

— J.S.